VENGEANCE VALLEY

ROCKY MOUNTAIN SAINT BOOK 8

B.N. RUNDELL

WOLFPACK
PUBLISHING
— EST 2013 —

Vengeance Valley
(Rocky Mountain Saint Book 8)
B.N. Rundell

Paperback Edition
© Copyright 2018 B.N. Rundell

Wolfpack Publishing
6032 Wheat Penny Avenue
Las Vegas, NV 89122

Paperback ISBN 978-1-64119-534-8
eBook ISBN 978-1-64119-533-1

Library of Congress Control Number: 2018963491

VENGEANCE VALLEY

CHAPTER ONE
WIND RIVERS

MAGGIE WATCHED THE BROAD SHOULDERS OF THE MAN sitting the Grulla gelding and taking the trail in front of her. She smiled with pride as she watched Tate's hips rock with the gait of the horse and the confidence of the man. This was the man who brought her into the Rocky Mountains on the search for her father, a would-be gold prospector that was lost to his family. And it was on that search that she found, not only her father but the love of her life who would become her partner. Riding beside the man was a youngster, pushing eleven, that resembled his father in every way. Confident, competent, and totally at home in the mountains, Sean had proven himself a quick learner and capable big brother to his sister, Sadie who was pushing six and now riding alongside her mother. The two redheads smiled at one another and Sadie asked the question, "How much longer, mother?"

It wasn't the first time that question came from the curious mind of her daughter, nor would it be the last. The family had traveled from their home in the Sangre de

Cristo Mountains, stopped in the Bayou Salado to visit Maggie's father who now lived with his wife Little Otter of the Yamparika Ute, and they were now on their way into the Wind River Mountains to a cabin Tate had built before he met Maggie.

"Well sweetheart, according to your father, not too much further. He said we're within shouting distance now. He said when we see the water of a lake, we'll be there."

"Good, I'm ready to walk and run, and not on a horse! It's been too long, and that's not counting the time we spent with Grandpa."

"I know Sadie, but we've had some fun, haven't we?"

"Uhhh, well, yeah. But I'm ready to sleep in a bed, like I had back home."

"You might have to wait on that a little, I'm not sure what we'll find in this cabin, but we can get you fixed up pretty soon, I'm sure." Maggie looked at Tate, who had reined up and sat waiting for her to come alongside.

He stepped down from his horse, held the reins of her buckskin as she dismounted, and when everyone was standing beside him, he turned around and said, "There it is!" and pointed to the dappled waters of a lake just below them. Black timber came down to water's edge on the far banks of the blue jewel in the wilderness. Two ravines held long stands of quakies, with their light green leaves shaking in the breeze, pointing up the mountainside to timber covered ridges and distant mountains. The same fingerprints of the Creator extended to the plains and on to the fading horizon in the east. The deep blue of the water told of its hidden depths and the smooth surface held the mirror image of the towering pines. Below them on the west shore to their left, the grassy shoulder of the mountainside sloped into the lake with a sandy edge.

Tate pointed to the shore on their left, "Back in the trees there, that's where the cabin sits. You can sit on the covered porch and see clear down to the lake." The family stood shoulder to shoulder, looking at their new home. Although this was a cabin Tate built several years back, this was the first time his family had come to the Wind River mountains.

It was in his fifth year in the mountains when the young man from Missouri came to the Wind Rivers and built a cabin for his new bride, White Fawn of the Arapaho. After Tate's mother died helping the Osage village fight small pox, and his father was killed by a crooked gambler, Tate was evicted from their home. The log home that had been provided by the school, his father being the only teacher. But it was an opportunity for the young man to head west to fulfill the long-held dream of exploring the far blue mountains that had been treasured by both son and father. After several years of exploring the Rockies, he rescued the young Arapaho girl from some renegade trappers and took her as his bride, after following his friend and mentor Kit Carson to a rendezvous in the Green River country. But White Fawn had fallen to pneumonia and her grave was behind the cabin in the tall pines above this mountain lake.

It had been close to a dozen years since Tate last came to the cabin, and now with his family, he was hopeful it still stood. If not, this was going, to be a very busy fall and his building skills would be put to the test. They mounted up and started back on the winding trail that would take them down the mountain and into the basin.

As they neared the clearing with the cabin, Tate reined up, motioned for the others to stop and be silent. He stood in his stirrups, leaned from side to side, and turned to speak quietly to Maggie, "There's smoke comin' from the chimney. I didn't see it from up yonder, so it might be somebody just started the fire. Could be just about anybody, but you and the young'uns wait here while I go find out."

Maggie nodded and motioned for Sean and Sadie to get down and hold their horses. The three stood stroking the horse's noses and speaking softly to them to keep them quiet and not give away their location.

As Tate rode into the clearing, he called out, "Hello the Cabin!" He stopped, waiting for a response from those inside. Lobo, Tate's constant companion and pet wolf, dropped to his belly beside the horse. Tate looked around, saw two horses in the corral behind the cabin, but nothing to indicate a long-term occupancy. He watched as the door cracked open and a voice called out, "Who you be?"

"I'm Tate Saint, and that's my cabin you're in."

The door opened wide to reveal a man almost as big as the doorway. With grease blackened buckskins, his shape was that of a barrel and most of his chest was obscured with black whiskers with a streak of white at one side. The whiskers covered his face and intertwined with thick eyebrows that shadowed eyes as black as coal. His hair shot out in all directions and seemed to reach the width of his shoulders. Tate could not help but stare at the half bear and half man. When he growled, his voice did little to change Tate's first impression, and the man asked, "You be Tate Saint? You the one they call Longbow?" His eyes dropped to the wolf that now stood and watched the man at the door.

"That's right," answered Tate, surprised the man knew of him.

A splash of color split the black whiskers and a belly laugh that sounded like water splashing at the bottom of a deep well accompanied the man as he stepped out on the porch and said, "Well, step down an' come on in, we just stopped for the night, like we done a'fore. Come on, and join us fer some stew. Muh woman's a mighty good cook!" he declared.

"I've got my family back there a piece," Tate started, but was stopped by the man's raised hand.

"That's fine, fine. Muh woman'd like the comp'ny. Bring 'em on and we'll share what we got."

Tate looked at Lobo, motioned for him to go back to the others, and dismounted. The big man came from the porch and extended his hand, "They call me Whiskers, an' I'm mighty proud to make your acquaintance." Tate grinned and shook the man's hand and the two walked together to the corral to unsaddle the Grulla.

"Yessir, me'n muh woman stopped here a couple times when we was down thisaway. We usually stay with her people, the Arapaho."

Tate looked at the man, "Your woman's Arapaho?"

Whiskers paused and examined Tate's expression, knowing that some white men had a problem with different or even all Indians, but he saw Tate's expression was one of curiosity and not anger. He answered, "That's right. We been together, oh, 'bout four or five years now."

"What band is she with? Who's their chief?" asked Tate as he stripped the gear from Shady. He swung the saddle and bags to the top rail of the corral, put the blanket atop the gear, and turned back to the big man.

"Uh, I cain't pronounce the name o' the band, it's like Basa somethin', but the chief is Red Pipe," he looked at Tate, "Why? Ya know them, do ya?"

"Oh, when I was in these mountains before, I knew some of them," he looked up as Maggie and the youngsters came into the clearing, leading the pack mules. He motioned them to the corral and helped them down, "Maggie, this is Whiskers."

The big man nodded his head, making his whiskers bounce, and bent slightly at the waist as if to bow. He grinned and said, "Mighty pleased to meet'chu ma'am. I ain't seen a white woman in years!" He looked to Tate and said, "You got'chu a mighty fine family here, yessir!" He turned back to Maggie, "Ma'am, if'n you're of a mind to, you can go on into the cabin there. Muh woman's fixin' up a pot a stew. Her name's Red Hawk, but she don' speak too much Amer'can."

Maggie glanced to Tate, who nodded, and she smiled as she turned and took Sadie's hand to walk to the cabin.

Sean helped his pa unsaddle the horses and Whiskers pitched in to help derig the mules. Tate had added another mule when they left the wagons at the Cochetopa and it was loaded with fresh elk meat taken the day before. Tate handed a big cut of haunch to Sean, "Son, how 'bout you takin' that in to your ma to add to the pot for supper?"

"Sure, Pa," replied the eager boy, staring at the log cabin tucked into the trees but showing the wide covered porch. A thin wisp of smoke twisted its way from the stone chimney, promising warmth within. The boy was especially anxious to see the cabin his father spoken of but never described, that would be their new home.

Whiskers watched the boy run toward the cabin and said, "Mighty fine lookin' boy, must make you proud."

As Whiskers looked toward the cabin, Tate turned to look up the slope toward the grave of White Fawn. He was pleased to see the marker still standing and the grass covering the site. A patch of purple and white columbines waved in the breeze and some scarlet Gilia stood tall nearer the pines. He breathed easy at the sight and turned back to the gear, stacking the packs at the edge of the lean-to shelter and out of the way.

Tate looked to Whiskers as the two men started toward the front of the cabin, "Been in the mountains long?"

Whiskers turned to look at Tate, smiled, and said, "Muh first year was at the Rendevous when you n' Kit married up with them two Arapaho women. The year Kit whupped that big ol' French trapper, Chouinard."

"You were there?" asked Tate, stopping to look at the man, surprised at his revelation. "I don't remember seeing you," he chuckled, "and you're not a man to miss!"

Whiskers chuckled as well and said, "Wal, I weren't this big then, didn't have these whiskers, an' there weren't no reason to remember me. I was just one o' the freighters that came out with Sublette. But I shore remember that fight!" he declared, shaking his head as he pictured the event still talked about in the mountains. "It was a doozy, that one were. After that, I hooked up with a couple fellers and thot I'd try trappin', but with the market fer beaver already goin' bad, I just went out on muh own, learned muh way 'round these mountains, found me a good woman, and here I be," he declared.

"Good a' place as any, I reckon," answered Tate, still surprised.

When they stepped up on the porch, Tate saw Sean and Sadie romping with Lobo and knew they were glad to be where they could stretch their legs. The men pushed through the door and stopped to watch the women, oblivious to their approach, talking in a combination of sign language, and a conglomeration of English, Shoshonean, and Arapaho. Maggie was very quick to learn other languages, but this was her first introduction to Arapaho. But the women didn't seem to have any difficulty communicating as their hands seemed to be flying and a muddling of words in different tongues blended to make both women smile and laugh with one another.

Whiskers looked to Tate, "Don't seem like they're havin' any trouble at'all. Just like wimmen, they can always find sumthin' to talk about."

Tate laughed and added, "Probably us!"

CHAPTER TWO
HOME

THE BIG BAY WOULD HAVE BEEN A SUITABLE PLOW HORSE ON any farm and was big enough to bowl over a buffalo, but with Whiskers aboard, the two appeared suited for one another. In the shadow of the big man, rode Red Hawk aboard a black mare that looked like a pup following its mother. For every feature that Whiskers and his mount had, the opposite was seen in his companion and hers. But the pair was complementary and had become a familiar sight in the Wind River Mountains, as Tate was soon to find out.

Maggie and Tate stood side by side, shoulders touching, as they watched their new friends take the trail through the black timber and away from the lake. Tate looked down at Maggie, "Whiskers said they were headed over to the summer camp of her people."

"I know, Niisih'eiht or Red Hawk told me. She also said she knew Waanibe and Nonooco, they were of her village, of the Bäsawunena people."

The two had turned back to the porch and Tate hesitated, looking at his redhead, "You're pretty quick about pickin' up the language. So, she knew them?"

"Yes, she said both Singing Grass and White Fawn were her friends. She also said you were, uh, how'd she say, yes, held in honor among her people."

"Hmmm, I guess I really didn't 'spect to be remembered, what with Little Raven gone. Didn't really think there'd be anybody left that I knew. But, I s'pose it ain't been all that long, although it does seem like a lifetime ago." He lifted his head and looked around and motioned toward the cabin and beyond, "But for now, I need to show you around the place, since this is gonna be our home fer awhile."

Maggie smiled and put her hand through his crooked arm and said, "Lead the way!"

It was nothing more than a simple walk around of the cabin and corrals as he talked about building them and the plans he had for adding on and improving, plans made and abandoned when he left. They stopped by the grave of White Fawn and were seated at the bench as Tate told Maggie more about the Arapaho girl and their time together. "It was different then, what with Kit and Waanibe gettin' hitched an' all, it just seemed like the thing to do. And it was a special time in our lives, we enjoyed the short time together, but," he turned to look at Maggie, "the Lord brought us together and it looks like you're stuck with me."

Maggie smiled and leaned against him, "Like glue, buddy, like glue!"

"Good! Cuz we got work to do!" He jumped to his feet

and led her to the tack shed beside the lean-to and picked up the larger pack and started to the cabin, "Well, get one an' come on!"

THE NEXT SEVERAL days were spent with Maggie busy in the cabin, cleaning, scrubbing, arranging, sorting, and doing all the things that only a woman can do to make a place a home, while Tate was busy outside. The corrals and lean-to needed repair, and high on his list was the building of a cache. Sean became his right-hand helper as they fetched several lodgepole pine for the making of the cache and the two worked well together. Sean was sent scurrying up the bigger of two tall spruce to tether a rope that would be used in the building and before long both father and son were mimicking a couple of squirrels, spending most of their time in the trees. But their efforts were rewarded when they stood on the ground and looked up at the cache box suspended between the two spruce. Made from the smaller lodgepole logs, the same as those used for tipi poles, it looked like a miniature cabin sitting atop two larger poles that had been secured to the two spruce. All the limbs below the cache had been cut away and the trunks of the two spruce had been given a band of axle grease about five feet from the ground and about a foot and a half wide, to prevent any bears or other varmints from climbing the tree to get at the cache. Tate had notched a single sizable pole to use as a ladder and a block and tackle for hoisting heavier items. With the cache measuring about five feet square, there would be ample space for storing their winter meat supply.

"Now we gotta go huntin' and get some meat to put in it, don't we Pa?" asked an eager Sean.

"Sure son, we'll be goin' soon 'nuff. There's plenty o' game in the area an' we shouldn't have any trouble fillin' that up. Let's go see how your nma and Sadie're doin', we might hafta give 'em a hand so they can fix us some supper, what say?"

"Sure Pa, I am gettin' kinda hungry."

Tate rubbed the boy's head, rumpling his hair as the two walked back to the cabin. They stepped over the little spring fed creek and followed the trail to the cabin. Sadie was sitting on the porch petting Lobo and looked up at her brother as he mounted the steps. "Ma said we could go swimmin'!" declared the girl excitedly.

"Oh, she did? When're we goin'?" asked Sean, looking to his sister and back to his pa.

"I don't know nuthin' 'bout it!" declared Tate as he shrugged his shoulders. "But, I'll go ask." He stepped past the youngsters and pushed through the door to find Maggie at the counter preparing their supper. He looked around the house and said, "I don't know how you do it, but this sure is nice!" He motioned to the many little things she had done to make the cabin look more like a home. The mantle over the fireplace had an arrangement of pine cones and drift wood, flowers were on the table that was covered with a buckskin with painted designs, the window above her counter had a curtain he recognized as coming from the skirt of a gingham dress, and other simple little items throughout that made all the difference.

Maggie turned around and wiped her hands on her apron and walked to her man with a smile and open arms.

"You are my home, you and those two out there on the porch." He bent and kissed her, and she wrapped her arms around his neck and kissed him back.

When they parted, he asked, "What's this about swimming?"

She giggled, "I thought that would be the easiest way for everybody to get a bath, don't you think?"

"If you think you're up to it, I s'pose we can do it. But you know, that water is mighty cold!"

"No excuses Mr. Tate Saint, you're gettin' a proper dunkin' just like the rest of us!"

WITH THE SHARPS rifle resting on his shoulder, his Colt Dragoon in its holster on his hip and his Bowie in the scabbard at his back, Tate followed Lobo and led the way for his family to the sandy shore of the lake. The inlet had pushed the sandy soil well into the lake and was marked by the cat-tails and scrub willows, but Tate chose a stretch of sandy shore that bordered a shallow area that had caught the day's sun and would be the closest thing to warm water they would find. With a finger of willows that pushed into the water, it would provide enough privacy for the girls as they tiptoed into the water amid gasps and squeals brought on by the cold snow-shed water. A stack of drift wood that had accumulated at spring run-off and high water provided a perch for Tate as he watched his family frolicking in the crystal-clear water. Sean had joined the girls but only until it was time to disrobe. They would scrub their clothes with lye soap once they were finished with the fun and they became accustomed to the temperature, but for now they splashed and waded in the shallow bay.

Tate let his eyes wander over the driftwood pile and reached down to pick up a chunk that he thought might be a good prospect for a little whittling, that he could maybe even make into a bowl for Maggie. He was focused on his search and it was a few moments before he noticed the silence. He froze, listening, and heard a quiet, almost whispered, "Tate, Tate, uh, Tate."

He stood to look over the willows and saw Maggie and the two youngsters, frozen in place, unmoving, and staring toward the bank. Tate instantly lifted his rifle as he turned to look at the edge of the willows, no more than thirty yards from the shoreline, to see a big mama grizzly standing and pawing at the air as she looked at these intruders into her domain. Behind her were two furball cubs, romping with one another as if nothing unusual was happening. Tate saw the big bear look his way and he dropped his face, but slowly lifted his eyes to watch but from an unthreatening posture. He spoke softly to his family, "Don't move, stay quiet."

The big bear looked over the group, tilted her head back and stretched open her mouth and bellowed a long roar obviously meant to intimidate. Then she dropped to all fours, pawed once at the air toward the family, roared again, turned to her cubs, and ambled back into the timber. As Tate sucked in a deep breath of relief, he turned to see his family visibly relax, and start toward the shore. "It's alright now, I'm sure she won't be back."

Maggie looked at the youngsters, "You two shuck outta them clothes and put this to work." She handed Sean a bar of Lye soap.

Maggie stood vigil as Tate got his 'dunking' and the family was soon on the way back to the cabin, clean bodies, clean clothes and all.

"Pa, would that grizz have come in after us?" asked Sean, as they walked towards the cabin.

"Well, son, you need to remember, the most dangerous critter in these mountains is a mama grizzly protectin' her cubs. Now, what do you think your ma woulda done if that grizzly came in the water after you?"

Sean looked at his ma and grinned, "She probably woulda taken after the grizz!"

Maggie and Sadie giggled at the thought, but Tate said, "Probably. And that's exactly what that ol' mama grizz was thinking. If she would'a thought her cubs were in any danger, she would have done anything to protect 'em, just like your ma. That's why she roared and clawed the air, she was tellin' us to stay away from her cubs."

"I thought you were gonna shoot her!" exclaimed Sadie.

"No, there was no need. We never kill any animals just to be killing. Now, if you're in danger, yeah, but if you're not hungry and not in danger, then let 'em be. They have just as much right to be in these mountains as we do, maybe even more so."

"Will they come back?" inquired the little girl, eyes flitting back and forth from the place where the bears disappeared to her father's expressive face, searching for reassurance.

"Well, this is their home too. But grizzlies cover a pretty big area and they don't like going where people are, so, I don't think we'll see 'em again. But, always be careful and watchful, and that's for anything, not just grizzlies," cautioned her father. They were at the cabin and the sun had dropped behind the mountains as they entered, wafted by the smells of supper in the pot at the fireplace.

It was a serene scene as they gathered around the table, held hands and prayed together. Each one took a turn and little Sadie said, "And God, thanks for protecting us from that big ol' grizzly, even though she was protecting her cubs, you protected us, an' you're bigger'n that ol' grizzly." The family chorused "amen" and dug into the elk pot roast and potatoes and squaw cabbage.

"THERE'S A WIDE-OPEN PARK JUST WEST OF US, UP ON TOP O' hills behind us. It's a good place to find some elk an' if we're lucky, we might get two or three and have a good start on our winter's cache, or at least enough for the rest o' summer," Tate explained as they were mounting up for the first hunt. Usually left to Tate or recently to Tate and Sean, this was to be a family hunt. Tate knew Maggie enjoyed hunting with him and he appreciated the time with her as well and it was about time for Sadie to be introduced into the reality of their meat source. Lobo was anxious and paced back and forth as he waited.

Although both Maggie and Tate had their Sharps rifles in the scabbard at their sides, Tate wanted them to use their bows. With the loud report of the Sharps, it was like announcing to anyone and anything within miles that they were there, and he preferred to keep their presence quiet. Sean had recently received a copy of his pa's English Longbow and had continually practiced with the weapon and was becoming quite proficient.

Tate's father, a school teacher and avid historian, had studied about the English longbow and taught Tate about the weapon. Their interest grew until they decided to try to copy the craftsmanship of the ancients and built a longbow. Once they became skilled, it was natural for them to build another and another until they had mastered the work. Tate's longbow was six feet tall and was fashioned from yew and cedar laminate and had a draw weight of about one hundred Kethirty pounds which, in the hands of a skilled archer, gave it an accurate and deadly range of a hundred and fifty yards and even further. This was easily three to four times the range and power of a traditional Indian bow. Sean's bow, although similar, was scaled to the boy and had the power more closely to that of an Indian bow, while his mother's bow was a gift from their friend, White Feather of the Comanche.

When Tate left Missouri after the death of his father, his preferred weapon was the longbow and his confrontation with a band of Kiowa hunters earned him the name of Longbow that he had become known by among many different tribes. Because of the size of the bow and the draw length, the arrows were six to twelve inches longer and the fletching was also longer to provide a more stable and accurate flight. Tate had downed buffalo and elk with the weapon and was confident in his ability to use it as easily and as accurately as a rifle. Until he recently acquired Sharps rifles for both himself and Maggie, he could easily shoot five or six arrows in the time it took to shoot a rifle and reload again. But the Sharps use paper cartridges and with the rolling block it could be fired eight to ten times in a minute.

The climb from the basin of the lake to the park above took a switch-back trail that wound through the thick timber and the early morning light struggled to pierce the crowded spruce and fir of the high country. The shadow marked trail was an ancient one used by animals and Indians alike for centuries and Tate looked at the gray and crumbling deadfall that had the signs of charcoal underneath that told of a forest fire long ago. Now the forest had re-grown and towered above them with spruce standing tall with trunks bigger around than the width of Tate's shoulders.

They broke into a grove of aspen and a red-headed woodpecker made his presence known as he hammered away on a tall snag and the sound echoed throughout as if he was warning everything of the intruders. Overhead a red-tailed hawk glided on an up-current, searching for his next meal and a low clucking from the fir told of a ptarmigan. The morning breeze whispered through the trees and the creak of the saddle leather and shuffling gait of the horses provided the only unusual sounds in the otherwise still forest.

As they neared the edge of the park, Tate led them to the side of the trail to dismount and tether their horses. Maggie and Sean slipped their quivers over their heads and one shoulder while Tate hung his from his belt at his side. He motioned for them to wait while he scouted the park and he stealthily crept through the trees to get a view of the park.

With several boggy areas hidden by low growing willows and buck brush, a clearing stretched across the basin that was crossed at the upper end by the Little Popo Agie Creek. Tallgrass waved in the breeze and as Tate stayed obscured behind a tall fir, he scanned the area. As he watched, a small herd of elk ambled from the trees and into the clearing. With the grass so tall and the brush, only the top edge of their backs and their long necks and heads showed. But when they dropped their heads to graze, it was difficult to see where or how many they were. Tate watched them move for a few moments, scanned the area for possible approaches, and returned to his family.

He explained his plan and before parting, he said to Maggie, "We'll give you two plenty of time to get into position before we do anything, but elk are creatures of habit and will probably go back the way they came, especially with us on the other side, so be ready."

Maggie smiled tolerantly at her husband and said, "Of course, you don't think I came all this way to take a nap, do you?" and giggled at her husband's expression.

Tate looked down at Lobo and said, "You go with her, and try to keep her outta trouble!" and motioned for him to follow. He watched as Maggie and Sadie started quietly through the timber. He knew it would take a little while, with all the downed trees from an apparent blow down in recent years, but he was certain she would make it to her position alright.

He motioned for Sean to join him and they started the opposite direction. They planned on a stalk from the other side of the park that would take them alongside the oak brush and into the willow covered flat by the grassy area. When they reached the edge of the trees, Tate stopped and nocked an arrow, and watched as Sean did the same. With a nod from his father, Sean led the way and started their stalk. They would be out of sight and downwind from the elk and the only thing that could give them away would be sound and Sean had proven himself to be a capable and quiet stalker.

Once in position behind the willows, they dropped to one knee and with only hand signs, Tate gave the youngster the go-ahead to prepare for a shot. While the boy readied himself, Tate bellied down to look beneath the willows and locate the best target. He rose back up beside his son and whispered into his ear, "There's a nice bull about fifteen yards that direction," he pointed through the brush, "and he's pointed thataway," he nodded toward the upper end of the park away from their position. "You step around this side and take your shot, I'll be right behind you."

Sean nodded to his father, slowly rose from his knee and in a slight crouch started around the edge of the brush. He mentally rehashed his father's instructions about the longbow, how the bow is pushed away from the body by stepping into it as compared to a traditional draw back of the string from an extended arm. Sean quietly and slowly took his position, only slightly obscured by extended willows, and stepped into his shot to quickly release the arrow. The muffled twang of the string came at almost the same instant as the arrow struck the bull, but the slight sound just before the impact startled the bull and he made a half-step before, making the arrow hit farther back on the rib cage. The bull stumbled but turned to take flight, startling the rest of the herd back toward the trees. With Tate at the ready behind his son, he quickly stepped into his bow and let fly his arrow. He had led the stumbling bull with his aim and the arrow found its mark just behind the foreleg and low in the chest, piercing the animal with its full length.

The bull took one more step and fell forward into the deep grass.

AS THE REST of the herd stampeded into the timber, Maggie waited with drawn bow and when her chosen target cleared the trees before her, she let fly with her arrow and it whispered to find its mark, causing the spike bull to stumble and fall. The other elk could be heard thundering through the timber to make their escape. A whistle from the clearing that mocked the shrill cry of the red-tailed hawk told Maggie that Tate and Sean were approaching.

SEAN FETCHED the horses while Tate and Maggie worked on the butchering. They skinned the elk, deboned the meat and used the hides to hold the big cuts of meat. Lobo supervised and did his best to down the many scraps and intestinal parts allowed him. With skilled and experienced hands, the work was soon done and loaded onto the two pack mules. After cleaning up in the stream, Tate stood and motioned for Maggie to be still and listen. In the distance, to the south, a muffled rumbling could be heard. Maggie looked at Tate, "Thunder?"

He scowled, and listened, then shook his head. The smattering of sound continued for a few moments, paused, and finally tapered off to stop. The chuckling of the stream had kept them from hearing the sound at its beginning, but now standing, they easily heard. Although it came from a considerable distance away, Tate knew how sound carried in the mountains, and he reckoned on the location of the unusual noise. He turned away and helped the youngsters aboard their horses and said to Sean, "Think you remember the way home?"

"Sure Pa, I can get us home!" and reined around his horse toward the trail down the mountain.

Maggie started to move out, looked back at Tate and asked, "What was it?"

"Rifle fire, and lots of it. That came from South pass."

She turned away, took a deep breath and gigged her mount to follow the youngsters, knowing that much fire did not bode well for anyone. She turned in her saddle to see Tate standing in his stirrups and waving. He hollered, "I'll be back as soon as I can. Keep the kids close and your rifle ready, I don't know what all this means, but I've got to find out."

CHAPTER FOUR
WAGONS

LOBO LED THE WAY ON THIS FAMILIAR ROUTE AND TATE knew it would take at least an hour to get there. The familiar trail climbed through black timber and he put Shady to a trot. The horse felt the tension and urgency as Tate's heels tapped his ribs. Tate was certain the gunfire came from South Pass and that it probably meant some freighters, or a wagon train had been attacked. South Pass was the only common ground for the Oregon, California, Mormon, and Emigrant trails with all of them coming over this pass and dividing after crossing the continental divide. The numbers of hopeful emigrants had continually increased since Benjamin Bonneville and the first wagon train made the crossing in 1832. The numbers didn't really increase until the late 1840's, early 1850's, and by that time the many emigrants moving to the west came through this pass. But now the many different tribes of Indians, Cheyenne, Arapaho, Ute, Crow, Shoshoni, were no longer complacent about the influx of settlers and many were rising up to stop the westward flow. That was what concerned Tate as he rode through the thicker timber of the south end of the Wind River Mountains.

The sun was high in the midday sky when he neared the edge of the timber. The flats at the top of the pass afforded little protection with scattered juniper, some cedar, but mostly thin grass and rocks. Even before Tate neared them, he could smell the acrid gunpowder and worst of all, burning flesh. He lifted his neckerchief to cover his nose and stepped down. He brought the Sharps hammer back, and with the long reins of Shady hanging over his crooked arm, he motioned Lobo to move out and he followed. The wolf moved in a stalk, eyes searching the area for any movement, any danger, lifting each paw and carefully placing it down, mirrored by Tate.

Smoke rose from some of the wreckage, the carcasses of the dead already drawing attention from the circling turkey vultures. Magpies and whiskey jacks danced about the debris, two coyotes tucked tail at the sight of Lobo and scampered away. Canvas bonnets were burnt or ripped apart. Trunks and boxes had been smashed open and contents strewn. The wagons were still strung out, showing they had no time to circle up for defense. Bodies, bloodied and mutilated, lay askew, eyes wide open in fear, silent screams coming from mouths agape. Most bodies had been stripped naked and mutilated, all had been scalped, even children. As Tate moved about the carnage, he looked for any sign of the attackers. There were a few broken lances, and many arrows, most broken but with the points removed to be reused. The fletching on some of the arrows appeared to be turkey feathers, common among the Cheyenne and Crow, whose villages were found in the flats. The Arapaho, Shoshoni, Ute, all mountain dwellers, preferred the feathers of eagles or hawks. But Tate knew the Cheyenne to be a peaceful people and seldom fought against whites.

He often paused to listen, to look for any movement, searching for any sign of life, but there was none. There was little of value or usable, with most items of any size having been heaped on a pile to be burned and still smoldering. The stench of burning flesh made him want to retch, but he fought it down, sighed heavily, and turned away to lean on the end of a wagon box, shaking his head at the carnage. His shoulders lifted as he drew a deep breath, choking on the smoke and stink, and began to search for a shovel or something to aid in the grisly task. He pushed at a smoldering box with his foot, saw the handle of a shovel protruding from beneath, and picked it up, wiping it free of ash and dirt.

He looked at the work to be done and stepped back aboard Shady to look for a burial site. Spotting a rocky slope, he rode to it to see if it would work and reined Shady around to return to the remains of the wagons. He estimated there were about thirty bodies, too many to dig individual graves, and decided to make a mass grave by the rocks. He looked Heavenward and muttered, "God, forgive me for not doin' more, but, well, you see how it is." He shook his head again, as he thought about these people, full of hopes and dreams, planning their tomorrows, and where they thought they would stop for a quick meal and a bit of rest, they would be buried with those same hopes and dreams unfulfilled.

Using a sideboard from a wagon as a sled, he piled several bodies on, used Shady to drag them to the rocks, rolled the bodies into the depression, and returned for another load. He did his best to show as much respect for the dead as he could, but the labor was difficult, the smell overwhelming, and he was alone. He found another spade under the edge of a broken-down wagon box, retrieved it and placed it atop the bodies to use later. He repeatedly had to chase off the carrion eaters; they were growing in numbers faster than he could carry the bodies. He returned for another load and was struggling to pull a body of a woman from underneath a wagon box when he was startled by a shouted, "What are you doing!" He fell back when he let go and looked to see a young man coming at a trot.

Tate jumped to his feet, put his hand on the butt of his pistol and asked, "Who are you?"

The young man with dark touseled hair, torn clothes and dirty face, appeared to be around fifteen, close to full grown, but still showing his youth. He had wide fearful eyes and tracks of tears down his cheeks, as he stared at the body of the woman. Without looking at Tate, he rasped, "That's my mother, what are you doing to her?"

"Easy boy, if this is your ma, she's long gone, like the rest o' these folks." Tate was compassionate, considering the boy's loss, but his weariness tempered his patience and with a glance at the sun to consider the remaining daylight, he added, "Now, you can help if you want, but they need buryin' and that's what I'ma doin'."

The boy looked at Tate, dropped his eyes to Lobo and stepped back, "That's a wolf!" He searched for safety, looking at the wreckage of the wagon and back at the wolf.

"Easy boy, he's with me, an' he won't hurt you long as

you behave. Now, what's your name? And is there anybody else with you? Anybody else that survived this?"

The boy looked at Tate, seemed to focus as he shook his head and said, "Uh, why?"

"Well, if there is, we need to get you some place safe. After we get this buryin' done, that is. So, what is it?"

"What is what?" asked the boy, confused.

"Your name, son, your name. Mine's Tate, Tate Saint, yours?"

He dropped his head, put his hand to his forehead and mumbled, "Ira, Ira Whitson."

"And are there any others?"

"Uh, yeah, just one." He lifted his eyes to Tate and answered, "I'll go get her, but she's hurt, could you help?"

"Sure, lead the way." Tate followed the boy into the trees on the south edge of the flats, where a large grove of juniper offered the only nearby shade. The boy pushed through the branches calling out, "Vicky? Vicky, I'm coming in and I have somebody with me." Their hideaway was a small opening among the thicker junipers and Vicky was sitting cross-legged, holding a handful of leaves on an apparent wound on her thigh. The blonde-haired girl lifted terrified eyes and tried to scoot back away as the two came near.

Tate looked at the frightened girl and spoke softly, "It's alright, I'm here to help. What happened to you?"

"A, a Indian came at me with a knife an' Ira shot him. Then we crawled away to these trees. He helped me," she said, nodding toward Ira.

Tate looked at the girl, her face white with fear but also from the loss of blood. He knew she needed tending and bent to look at the wound. He asked, "May I see?"

She looked to Ira who nodded, and back to Tate and lifted her hand. When she lifted the leaves, the blood flowed from a deep wound and trailed down her thigh into the pool beside her. Tate placed her hand back on the wound and said, "I'm gonna carry you outta here. We've got to get you fixed up an' I've got some stuff in my saddle bags." He slipped an arm behind her, the other under her knees, and lifted her as he stood and motioned for Ira to push the branches aside. As he walked from the trees, he looked around and instructed Ira, "Go to that sage over yonder," nodding his head toward a scraggly cluster of blue-tinted brush, "and peel off a bunch o' them leaves. Then go over there to that bunch of tall pink flowers," again nodding, "an' pull up some of 'em and get the roots."

He carried the girl to where Shady stood ground tied by the remains of a wagon and Lobo lay beside him. When he sat the girl in the shade of the wagon, she spotted Lobo and stiffened, "There's a-a-a wolf!" Lobo came to his feet and to the side of Tate and dropped to his belly. She looked at the wolf, and back at the man and said, "Is he safe?"

Tate reached out and rubbed behind Lobo's ears and said, "Sure, long as you behave he's fine. Been with me a long time, best friend I've got. Now, let's look at that leg again."

WITH THE POULTICE from the sage leaves and the fireweed root, Tate bound the leg with a wide patch of buckskin and long strips to keep it tight. He gave the girl some water and some pemmican and returned to the task of burial with Ira helping. Once all the bodies were collected and put in the depression, he used the spade and the nearby rocks to cover them and with Ira beside him, he recited a portion of Psalm 37, *Fret not thyself because of evil doers, neither be thou envious against the workers of iniquity. For they shall soon be cut down like the grass, and wither as the green herb. Trust in the Lord, and do good; so shalt thou dwell in the land, and verily thou shalt be fed.*

He bowed his head and prayed a simple prayer of commitment for the dead and to ask for guidance and protection for those that remained. When he said "Amen," the boy looked up at him and asked, "Do you really believe that? That part about evil doers gettin' what's comin' to 'em?"

"Of course, I believe everything in the Bible, don't you?"

Ira looked back at the wagons, and answered, "I don't know, I used to, but now, I just don't know."

"Well, let's see if we can get you and your friend back to my cabin and get you fixed up a mite, reckon?"

"Don't have much choice, do we?"

When they returned to Vicky, she had passed out and slumped over. Tate looked at her and asked the boy, "Think you can ride my horse and hold her in the saddle? I'll be there with you, but my horse can't pack all three of us."

"Sure, I can hold her." Riding double was nothing new for a boy from the country. When there were more kids than horses, it was common for two and more to ride together on the youthful adventures. The memories of a worry-free childhood clashed with the reality of this day and he wondered if he would ever know those days again.

. . .

Twilight was fading when Tate and company came into the clearing by the house. Maggie was sitting on the porch waiting and when they neared she came down the steps, "Now, how'd I know that you would be bringing some-body home with you?" she grinned and looked up at the two tired and dirty young people. Vicky was still uncon-scious, and Tate lifted her down to carry her into the house as Maggie led the way and opened the door.

THE BINNÉESSIIPPEELE, RIVER CROW, OF THE APSÁALOOKE people had gathered a council. The largest tipi in the camp held a small fire in the center and the many warriors, elders, and leaders were seated in rows that encircled the fire. The ceremony of the pipe concluded, and Káamneewiash, Blood Woman, addressed the circle.

"We of the River Crow stand alone against all others. When the Mountain Crow signed the treaty with the white soldiers, our leaders walked away. We have fought against the Lakota, the Arapaho, and the Cheyenne. We did not take this fight to the whites, but they have taken our lands, our buffalo, and more. Are we women that we do not fight?"

Those that agreed shouted war cries, or grunts or other sounds to show their agreement as Blood Woman was seated. He stared at the fire as others muttered among themselves. Another leader, Chíischipaaliash or Rotten Tail, stood and the others quieted.

"Blood Woman speaks with power. He has shown this

Xapáaliia, medicine, in battle and as he leads our people. When the Mountain Crow signed, our fathers left. When the whites again wanted us to sign, the Mountain Crow and the Kicked in the Bellies Crow signed, but our leaders walked. Now the whites come in herds as great as the buffalo. Can we fight against such numbers? Will they not run us over as a herd that runs in fear? Their weapons are great, their numbers are many." Again, the response of shouts and murmurs, some even stomping their feet, and many speaking at once.

Another man rose, he was not a chief as the others, but he was a respected and prominent warrior. Uuwatchi-ilapish, Iron Bull, raised his hands to silence the circle.

"Our grandfathers tell of the spotted disease that showed with running sores and came upon our people from the whites, many died a painful death with no weapon in their hands. Our fathers tell of other diseases, that of spots and that disease that empties our bodies of all things, brought by the whites. Then they come in great numbers and take our buffalo. Our hunt that sends the buffalo off the cliff and gives our people meat for the long cold days, was stopped by the many whites in their wagons that turned back the herds. What must they do before we act?"

Iron Bull had reminded his people of the plagues brought by the white men. From the 1837 smallpox epidemic through the lesser epidemics of measles, typhus, cholera and other diseases, the number of natives of all tribes that fell to these plagues exceeded a hundred thousand deaths. With no natural immunity, the Indians died of the diseases of the white man and the epidemics took on a life of their own, passing from tribe to tribe and back again. These were pestilences beyond measure and continually raised the anger of the native peoples.

Most of those in the back circles, the younger warriors that ached for vengeance shouted, stood and stomped their feet and yelled their war-cries. But Iron Bull, still standing, raised his hands again, "Our warriors want to go into battle. They want to drive the whites from our land. One of our war leaders, Daasítchileetash, Bad Heart Bear, led some of our warriors against some of these wagons and destroyed them. Those that would come into our land, take our buffalo, poison our water, destroy our ways, have been stopped!"

Iron Bull sat down, nodding to those around him, and the raucous response of the younger warriors took a few moments to subside. Rotten Tail raised his hand, stood, and began, "Each man must do as he believes Akbaatatdia, the Creator, would have him do, but it must be true medicine, from the Creator. Then all will know diakaashe, He really did it. But, if you do this in your own power, you will bring judgment upon all our people."

The words of Rotten Tail struck to the core of the beliefs of the Crow people. These that made the people who they are, and everyone present grew quiet. The gray-haired elders nodded their heads, chiefs grunted their agreement, and the circles stilled. Blood Woman spoke without rising, "We will think on what has been said, we should seek our Creator and come together again."

The humbled group slowly stood and filed from the hide lodge, leaving the chiefs behind to further discuss what the River Crow people would do and who would take the lead. But while the wise ones considered, the young warriors were gathering near the lodge of Bad

Heart Bear. Bear, now a proven leader, had risen in respect among his warriors. When any leader of a raid was successful he gained honors and the more honors, the more others were willing to follow. When he led the attack against the wagons at South Pass, he had twenty-three warriors with him, but now more wanted to follow him. While the old ones discussed what would be best for the people, the exuberance of youth showed itself among the eager warriors as they gathered near Bear's lodge.

"Aiiieee, while the old women talk, the whites take our lands. We must go against them!" declared Holds the Enemy, Bear's close friend and ally.

"Yes! When we shed their blood and take their scalps, others will be too afraid to come!" shouted Crazy Fox.

Pretty Eagle, a respected warrior that had taken many coups and held many honors spoke, "Our people need meat more than scalps! What will you do for the people? What good are honors if the people starve?"

Bad Heart Bear stood, "Our brother, Pretty Eagle, is right," he paused while others grumbled, "and we must get meat for our people. But if the whites drive away the buffalo what are we to do? I tell you what we do, we go for the buffalo to get meat for our people and if any whites are in the way, we kill them!" he shouted. Those nearby repeated their cries and shouts, attracting others. When more gathered, Bear again spoke, "This night, we will go to the south to take the buffalo for our people. When we bring meat to our village, others will want to come with us and we will have many warriors to go against the whites! We can get both meat and scalps! Who will go with Bad Heart Bear?" he shouted and was answered by all those that stood nearby.

The vengeance seekers knew each warrior must make his own choice and decide for himself who to follow, for among the Crow, as with most of the native peoples, there is not a hierarchy that demands obedience to a spoken command. But when the council of leaders made a decision for the well-being of the people, then all are expected to follow that lead. When a warrior leader elects to go on a raid or a hunt, anyone can join but if that action is contrary to the decision of the council, that warrior and any who follows, risks being cast out of the village in disgrace. When Bad Heart Bear put together his hunting and raiding party, he purposefully did so before the decision was made by the council, so he would not be obligated to abide by their decision. His lust for blood and battle and the honors that would bring goaded him into that action. But this decision could bring his downfall and perhaps his death and the death of many of his warriors. Yet the belief in the invincibility and strength of youth had driven many a young man to his death.

CHAPTER SIX
RECOVERY

WHEN SHE OPENED HER EYES, THE FIRELIGHT SHOWED THE still form of her friend sleeping on a bedroll to the far side of the fireplace. Vicky looked around and was surprised to see the interior of a cabin with table and chairs, shelves stocked with goods, a curtained window, all the fixings of a home. She remembered the attack on the wagons and her escape with Ira, then something about a man that came to help. She reached under the blanket to feel her leg and her fingers touched the bandage and the soreness of the wound on her thigh caused her to wince. She pushed the blankets back and sat up to look around some more when a door opened, and a woman came out.

MAGGIE SAW her patient was sitting up and she whispered, "Oh, you're awake. Good. I came to check your bandage, and to see if you needed something. Food maybe? Or something to drink?"

"Where am I?" asked Vicky.

"Oh, I'm sorry, I'm Maggie. My husband, Tate, brought you and Ira back from the wagons. You've been out of it for a while, but it's good to see you awake." She walked to the side of the girl and knelt beside the pallet of blankets, "May I look at the bandage?"

"Uh, yeah, I guess so. It's awful sore."

Maggie loosed the wide buckskin strips and carefully lifted the larger piece of buckskin that held the poultices in place. By the light of the fire, she looked at the wound, smiled, "Oh, it looks fine. You're going to be up and around in no time." She stood and went to the table for more of the poultice compound and returned to replace the bandage. She sat back on her heels and looked at Vicky, "Now, would you like something?"

"Maybe some water, please?"

TATE SAT on his bench by the tall fir and looked at the mirror surface of the lake below. The pink light of early morning painted the bottom of some scattered clouds, and the image was reflected on the water. Nothing stirred, even the nighthawks dozed, and the wind no longer whispered in the pines. This was the time of day Tate enjoyed most, as he shared the time with his Lord in prayer. Sometimes he spoke the words, other times a quiet whisper escaped from his spirit, and other times it was merely the thoughts and that still small voice heard deep within that gave communion with his Master and Savior. Tate was concerned, the carnage of the wagons crowded into his memory and he remembered other trains of settlers, people who had become his friends and were determined to fulfill their dreams. People not unlike those that now lay buried beside the pinnacle of South Pass.

He moved his family to the Wind River mountains from the Sangre de Cristo range far to the south. The Comanche, Apache, and Ute Indians, although many were his friends, all seemed to be growing restless. Treaties were made and broken; the whites wanted to move the native peoples off their lands and confine them to reservations, and those attempts were being met with resistance. When the Mouache Ute and the Jicarilla Apache allied together and attacked Fort Pueblo on Christmas day and massacred everyone, it threatened to become a rallying cry for all to band together and fight against the encroachment of the whites. Because of that, Tate brought his family north to the Wind River mountains. But now, he saw the same things beginning to happen.

Tate had been taught to always try to see and understand both sides of any disagreement. His compassionate mother died trying to help the Osage Indians fight an epidemic of smallpox. His teacher father was killed by an unscrupulous gambler. But Tate always tried to see the other side. Perhaps he had too much empathy, but he could understand and even agree with the argument of the natives.

They had been lied to, cheated, and massacred, and in turn they did the same to the white man. It would have been easy for Tate to view the Indian as a barbarian and an animal like those whites that thought all Indians should be killed. But he had known Indians of several different tribes, befriended most, and helped many. It was easy for him to learn they were just people with different beliefs and culture. And the better he knew them, the more he understood their beliefs were not all that different from his own. The native peoples had strong family ties and a belief in a Creator as well as a confidence in life hereafter more than many whites. But most pilgrims did not want to understand the ways of a people that had lived for decades perhaps centuries in this wild and savage land. Most only saw the Indian as an obstacle to overcome.

But there were those Indians, renegades many of them, that were as bad or worse than the whites that wanted to obliterate them and sought only to destroy and drive the intruders from their lands. He believed it was a band of Crow warriors that had attacked the wagons and he remembered it was also a band of Crow that had attacked the Arapaho and killed his friend, Little Raven, and many others. What he wanted to know was if these attacks were a part of a bigger Indian war, and if so, was his family in danger?

He sighed heavily and started to rise when Maggie put her hand to his shoulder and sat beside him. Her rosy complexion with the parade of freckles across her nose and her red hair that fell in curls shone a little brighter in the pink glow of the sunrise, and he smiled as he slipped his arm around her shoulders. She leaned against him and they sat quietly for a few moments, enjoying the stillness of the morning together.

She lifted her eyes to him and said, "The girl's awake. Her leg wound looks good, but I don't know about her mind. That was an awful thing for a young woman, or a young man, to witness. And we don't know about their families, I mean, if they have any family besides those in the wagons."

"Well, we'll find out soon enough. No since pushin' 'em, making 'em think they gotta leave or anything. Course, I don't know what we're gonna do if they don't have some place to go."

"Well, instead of being concerned about tomorrow, how about some breakfast for today?"

"Now you're talkin' my language. Lead on, I'm right behind you," declared Tate as he rose from the bench to chase after his wife who already had a head start.

TATE WAS BELLY DOWN on the grassy creek bank as he showed Sean and Ira how to hand fish. They were just below the confluence of two runoff streams that fed the lake below and just in the trees below the trail that came from South Pass. "Now, you cup your hand like this," he demonstrated, "kinda like when you carry your rifle loosely. Then you slowly put it down near the bank. Ya see, here at the bend, the current kinda washes out under and the trout like to lay back in there an' wait for some bit o' grub to float their way. Now, if you slowly bring it up against the current, you'll be able to feel any fish layin' in there." He slowly moved his hand, with the water depth between his elbow and shoulder, "and when you feel one, just slide it up under and slip it forward to the gills, grab hold, and pull 'em out!" He rolled to his side, bringing up a nice sized trout and tossed it on the grass. Before the others could get to it, Lobo had it in his mouth and had chomped down on what he thought was his dinner, to the howls of the others.

"Well, anyway, that's how you get one. Just knowin' that might keep ya' from goin' hungry in these mountains!" declared Tate, as he laughed along with the two youngsters. Tate sat back on the grass, wiping off his wet and very cold arm, and pushed the sleeve of his buckskin shirt down to warm his arm. He froze in place and cocked his head as he motioned for the boys to be quiet. Lobo had come to his feet and looked toward the trail that was slightly obscured in the trees as Tate reached for his rifle. The sound of hooves on the rocky ground alerted them of someone's approach, but Tate listened and was certain there was only one. He motioned to Lobo to go forward, but wait, and the wolf padded through the brush and trees, stopped and waited. Tate motioned for the boys to drop behind the brush to take cover and he stepped toward the trail.

With a sizable spruce between him and the trail, Tate saw a dapple-gray horse picking his steps on the trail, ridden by a white man in buckskins, with a Sharps rifle cradled behind the pommel. Tate called out, "Whoa up there!" The horse's head came up and the man reined the animal to a stop. He lifted his free hand, keeping one on the Sharps and answered, "I'm friendly, don't mean no harm. Lookin' for Tate Saint. That be you?"

"What do you want with him?" asked Tate.

"A skinny little runt by the name of Kit Carson told me to look you up!"

Tate stepped from behind the tree with his rifle still at the ready and said, "You found him. Step down."

The lanky lean man with long reddish blonde hair and

neatly trimmed facial whiskers grinned and swung a leg over the horse's rump and walked toward Tate, hand extended to shake. "I'm Jim Baker, scoutin' fer General William Harney outta Fort Laramie. Knowed Kit from a long time back an' he said if'n I was ever in the area, to stop by an' say howdy."

Tate took his hand and said, "Good to meet you. Heard 'bout you a time or two." He turned to holler to the boys, "Come on out an' meet this feller."

The boys didn't bother to be quiet as they came through the trees, but Lobo came around behind and was shielded from view by the man. But when the horse caught his scent, he side-stepped quickly, turning his head back to see the wolf. The move startled the man and Baker stepped back when he saw Lobo then looked to Tate. When he saw Tate and the boys were smiling, he knew the wolf had to be with them and he turned to pat his animal's neck and talking softly in his ear.

Tate chuckled and said, "That there's Lobo, but these two young'uns are Sean, he's my son, and Ira. Picked him an' a friend of his up on South Pass a couple days back."

The group started toward the cabin and Baker said, "I saw the ruins of a wagon train. He from there?"

"Ummhumm, him an' a girl at the house."

As they neared the cabin, Tate called out, "Comp'ny comin'!"

Maggie pushed the door open and came onto the porch, smiling and wiping her hands on her apron. She shaded her eyes to look at the four coming toward the cabin and answered, "Well, wash up, supper's 'bout ready!"

She turned and went back into the house, chuckling to herself. When she entered, she spoke to Vicky, "That man, here we are in the middle of nowhere, high up in the mountains, no neighbors, and yet he finds somebody to bring home to supper." She laughed and smiled, "That's just his way."

CHAPTER SEVEN
DECISION

"M'AM, THAT GOOSEBERRY PIE WAS AN UNEXPECTED pleasure, I must say. And I'm thankin' you for it." Baker turned to Tate and said, "With cookin' like that, I'm surprised you don't weigh three hundred pounds." He chuckled at his own remark as did Tate and Maggie.

"Well, I do enjoy her cooking," replied Tate as he winked at Maggie.

Baker leaned his elbows on the table and asked, "So, how many were in them wagons?"

"Near as I could tell, 'bout thirty. Some were burnt and maybe some were nothin' but ashes, so . . . " he shrugged his shoulders at the memory.

"Could ya' make out who done it?"

"Prob'ly Crow. The few arrows with fletching had turkey feathers, an' sometimes them Crow also like blue markin', they took their dead, so, don't really know for sure," surmised Tate.

"That's all we need," drawled Baker, dropping his head and leaning back in the chair, scowling.

"Why? What else's goin' on?"

"Wal, the general down to Laramie sent me on this scout cuz o' the problems with the Mormons. They done run ol' Bridger off an' took over his tradin' post an' they been causin' other problems with some folks that ain't Mormon that's been travelin' through their territory. What with all that goin' on, there's some o' the higher ups are wantin' the army to move against 'em. I'm thinkin' the general's gonna be sendin' some troops thisaway fer 'em to move into Mormon country and set 'em straight. But, if we got Injun trouble goin' on, we won't have 'nuff troops to try to protect them wagons full o' settlers an' take on them Mormons too!"

"I see what you mean."

Baker looked down at his moccasins, took on a contemplative look, and lifted his eyes to Tate, "I'm wonderin' if we could get'chu to do some scoutin' fer us? The army'd pay ya', course it's a little slow in comin', but they'd pay ya."

"Just what're you thinkin'?"

Baker leaned on the table again and his eyebrows lowered to shade his eyes and he looked at Tate, "If you was to scout out them Injuns whut hit them wagons, you know, foller up on 'em, find out if it's just a bunch o' rene-gades or if it's all of 'em. So's we'd know if we was facin' the whole Crow nation or just a war party o' young bucs. That-a-way the general'd know better what to do with his troops. He's been hopin' he wouldn't hafta worry 'bout 'em none."

"Well, I'll admit I was thinking about doing that anyway, cuz I was wantin' to know if my family was in any danger, but how'd I get the word to ya?"

He leaned back in the chair, crossed one leg over the other and with his hand on his ankle, he looked up, "I'll be goin' down to Fort Bridger to scout that out, an' it'll take, oh, ten days, no more'n two weeks, an' I'll stop back by here. But," and he paused, looked to Maggie busy at the counter with the clean-up, "You also need to know, we got word there's been a couple other attacks. We heard of some trappers and hide hunters gettin' hit, onliest one that survived wasn't in camp, out runnin' a line, and he came into the Fort sayin' Injuns killed the whole bunch, eight of 'em. An' there's been word that some Arapaho had a run-in, an' a couple o' prospectors done in, too."

Tate stood and motioned for Baker to follow him outside. Once on the porch, the men glanced at the two youngsters romping in the clearing with Lobo and one another, the two men moved on to the corrals behind the cabin. Tate leaned his forearms on the top rail and looked to the tall mountain man, "I'll prob'ly do it, but I'll need a couple days to get ready. I want my family to be prepared, and with these two from the wagons, I don't know if they'll be a help or a problem. My woman can take care of herself and the young'uns, for that matter both Sean and Sadie are pretty handy with both rifle and bow, but if a bunch o' renegades attacked, well . . ."

"I understand. An' you're right to be concerned, I would be too."

Tate looked at the man, knowing he had been in the mountains many years and was respected by both Indians and other mountain men. "So, what do you think is behind all this?"

Baker looked up the mountain, back to Tate, and said, "If it was just a little scrap, I'd say it were a band o' young bucs lookin' fer honors, you know, coups, stealin' some horses, mebbe gettin' a few scalps. But I'm thinkin' this is shapin' up to be more'n that. I dunno if it's gonna be an all-out war, but there's some unhappy Injuns an' I think they're out fer vengeance."

Tate nodded, dropped his head and scuffed his moccasins in the dirt, "And who's leadin' 'em could make all the difference."

"Ummmhmmm," answered the scout. Both men grew somewhat contemplative, knowing what an all-out war with the Indians could mean.

"THAT LOOKS DIFFICULT," observed Maggie as she looked over Tate's shoulder at his work on the lapboard before him. Tate was knapping some shards of obsidian into arrowheads, tedious work and difficult. He grunted and continued. He paused, looked back to Maggie and said, "I'm thinkin' a little different. I'll make the arrow shafts black with charcoal and oil, add some white bands, and with black arrowheads, no one'll be able to tell where they come from or who made 'em. Most Indians are what you might call, notional. Anything they don't understand they get notions, or ideas about. They're almighty fond of what they call 'medicine' or power or what white men just call luck, an' anything they don't understand, they think might affect their medicine, especially if it comes with somethin' bad happenin', like one o' their braves gettin' kilt."

"So, why black?"

"Crow warriors, when they do somethin' special, kill an enemy, count coup, or somethin' like that, they paint their faces, sometimes more, all black to show they done somethin'. But black is also the color of death, an' if it scares 'em a little, then . . . " he shrugged his shoulders to let her imagination take over.

SHADY WAS GEARED up with loaded saddle bags, bedroll with a parfleche secured atop behind the cantle of the saddle, Sharps rifle in the scabbard under the fender leather on the right side, longbow in a sheath under the fender on the left side, and full quiver of arrows beside the saddle bags. After a long embrace with Maggie, Tate stepped aboard, lifted his eyes to the rising moon in the east that was waxing full, and said, "I don't know how long this'll take, but I know you can handle things here."

Maggie nodded and said, "You just take care of yourself and come home soon."

He nodded his head and reined Shady toward the trail. Tate preferred traveling at night whenever possible, the entire journey from Missouri to the mountains was made by the stars and he was one with the darkness. The trail of the Indians that hit the wagons would be his starting point and with a moon near full, and a clear night, he was confident he could follow, even though it was almost a week old.

On his first visit to the wagons, Tate had made note of the trail taken by the attackers when they left the area, and he turned to cut through the timber to intersect that route. The trail he sought was one that came from the mountains into the flats but took an indirect route, holding to the cover of the forest where possible and the contours of the land or geographic anomalies where timber was scarce. In a short while, he came to the trail

and readily found the tracks of the attackers. He estimated the war party to number close to two dozen, and
that many horses left a very visible trail.

When the attackers saw themselves as predators rather
than prey, they seldom bothered to cover their tracks,
believing themselves to be invincible and in no danger of
pursuit. That attitude was evident when he saw tattered
pieces of clothing and other objects taken from the
wagons and cast aside when deemed of no practical use or
value. Those things taken in the heat of battle or during
the pillaging of the remains, when seen in the light of day
or with the sober minds in the aftermath, are often
cast aside.

Tate paid little attention to the scraps and debris,
staying on the trail and vigilant of that which lay before
him. Lobo trotted easily along the trail and searched the
shadows for anything of concern. They kept a steady
pace, a fast walk, and covered distance easily. Lobo
stopped and sat at the side of the trail and Tate reined up
beside the wolf. They were at the edge of a cluster of scattered juniper and a slope that overlooked the long
rimrocked ridge of the red canyon. They would be in the
open for at least a mile or more with only the rise and fall
of the land to provide cover. In the pale of the clear night,
they could easily be seen, if anyone was watching. Tate
lifted his eyes to the sky, judged the time to be just after
midnight, and motioned Lobo onward.

They had already crossed a long rimrock ridge and a
dry lake and the many rocky hillocks that arrayed the
foothills, but now they faced a bald slope with nothing
but sage and bunch grass for cover, and little of that.
Before them, and stretching to the north, was the long red

rocked canyon wall above the valley of red clay. But in the moonlight, it showed only as a ragged shadow that scarred the plains before them. Tate knew the ridge was cut by the Little Popo Agie Creek and that cut held the oft-used trail that led into the wide valley of the Wind River. The Wind River flowed from high in the Rockies where the Wind River Range and the Absaroka Range nodded to one another across the valley of the Wind. Those mountains were the home of the Shoshoni, Arapaho, and Gros Ventre Indians with each tribe intent on defending their chosen territory and hunting grounds. But the valley of the river at the south end of the Absaroka and west toward the Bighorns was the land claimed by the Crow and Tate was riding into that valley.

Lobo ranged well ahead of Tate and moved easily in the flats, always going side to side, sniffing, searching, looking, listening, as if he was looking for his dinner, but more, he was looking for the war party. Once Tate put him on the trail, Lobo knew what he was after and moved anxiously but stealthily and with his dark gray, almost black, coat and the dim shadows of the sage and bunch grass, he was almost invisible.

When the trail dropped off a slight shoulder and neared the willows and alders that lined the small creek in the bottom of the one-sided canyon, Lobo stopped and settled down on his stomach to await Tate. As the man approached, he saw Lobo down and waiting and knew there was nothing hidden in the shadows of the brush. When he stopped beside the wolf, he saw the remains of the campsite of the Indians. He sat easily in the saddle and looked around by the light that showed silver, seeing the place of two campfires, where they tethered their horses, and where they bedded down. A scrap of light color near the brush caught his eye and he stepped down, ground tied Shady, and walked toward the sight, pistol in hand.

Thrown under the edge of the willows was the bloody rags of a woman's dress. Laying splayed and mutilated near the brush was the body of a white woman, streaks and spots of blood appearing black in the moonlight, her scalped head disfigured by the animals that had fed on her carcass. Tate turned away and went to Shady, picked up the reins and led the horse with Lobo following, several yards downstream away from the gruesome sight. With the gray light of dawn starting to chase the stars from the sky, he would make his camp here, get some rest, and bury the body before continuing his search.

CHAPTER EIGHT
SEARCH

HE COVERED THE GRAVE WITH RANDOMLY SPACED STONES, not wanting the grave to be obvious in the event the Crow returned on this trail. With no evidence of the body, they would only assume animals had carried off the remains, but a grave would tell them some white man had found the body and buried it. Tate didn't want any of the war party to suspect they were known. He obliterated any sign of his camp and mounted up as the twilight faded, to resume his search.

He followed the red rock ridge along the bottom of the valley, crossed the Little Popo Agie and when the trail rose out of the valley to a flat top butte, he slowed and let Lobo scout the area. In a short while, the wolf returned, and Tate swung aboard Shady to follow Lobo across the butte and down the finger ridge that took them to the grassy draw of the Popo Agie creek. He could tell by the direction of the tracks, the warriors were bound for a specific destination, probably their village at the summer camp.

He chose to hold to as much cover as possible, even though traveling at night. If he could see the trail, he could be seen, if he wasn't careful. With Lobo staying on the track, it was easy for him to travel away from the trail and keep to the trees or brush, anything that would obscure his silhouette. The Cicadas stayed busy with their scratchy rhythmic sounds, bullfrogs in the sloughs bragged about their prowess, and nighthawks sang their challenges to the stars. In the distance, he heard some coyotes sing their love songs, and once, he heard an owl ask his question of the darkness. If he was just traveling to see the country, he would enjoy the sounds of the night, but this was a mission of discovery and perhaps retribution, nothing to be enjoyed.

They crossed a dry point of land and dropped into another swale that carried a stream through the willows and alders and cottonwoods. After wading the shallow stream, the trail rose to cross a rolling flat scarred by several dry creek beds before coming to the wider valley of the Wind River. This was a floodplain where the river split and meandered, leaving bogs full of cattails and frogs, and wide stretches of shallow muddy stream with sandy bottoms. Tate and company easily crossed the low river and were soon confronted by a long line of adobe and alkali finger ridges and draws that came from a wide low flat-top mesa.

When the trail turned to climb the dry run-off arroyo, Lobo stopped to wait for Tate. The wolf stood alert, looking to the top of the low ridge, and Shady looked with ears forward, eyes wide, attentive to Lobo's bearing. Tate stepped down, looked from Lobo to Shady, and always in the habit of paying close attention to his animals' concerns, he looked and listened. The night sounds continued without interruption, but then he caught it, the slight smell of woodsmoke. There was a camp nearby. He ground tied Shady, slipped his bow from the sheath, hung his quiver on his belt and with a hand motion started Lobo up the slope.

As they neared the crest, Tate hunkered down, and then to his hands and knees, he crawled to the edge. On his belly, he scanned the flat before him. There was nothing close by, but he searched the flat, saw a dry creek bed that cut across and just below a small hill at the far edge. With nothing before them, Tate rose and started at a trot to the draw, Lobo at his side. Staying low and in the dry creek bed, they made their way to the hill and after a quick scan, rose from the draw and started up the hill.

As they neared the crest, he bellied down and both Lobo and Tate crabbed to the top to look into the valley beyond. A sizeable lake, one that Tate was familiar with as being rather shallow for a lake, but with low growing brush and a few cottonwoods surrounding the body of water, it was an excellent summer camp area. Below the hill but closer to the lake was the Crow village that numbered about a hundred lodges; a large camp by any measure, and undoubtedly one that was situated for the summer migration of buffalo. And the flats that surrounded the site also made it difficult for any enemy to mount an attack. The only high ground was where he now lay and that behind him.

He looked down at Lobo and whispered, "Well, boy, we found 'em, but now we gotta get us a place to camp before daylight catches us up here in plain sight of them Crow." They slid back from the crest and retraced their steps to the waiting Shady. When they were following the trail to this place, Tate, as any experienced man of the mountains would do, watched for places to find cover and places to camp. When they dropped into the valley of the Wind River, he had spotted just such a place. A dry creek bed that had been carved by big run-offs cut the high bank of the river after carving its way through a high-walled and winding sandstone canyon. It would provide them a well-hidden campsite and there would probably be some good grass, maybe even spring water for Shady.

His choice proved to be an excellent one and made a comfortable camp that could only be seen by someone standing at the top of the sandstone bluff and looking straight down into the deep draw and that was very unlikely. By the time Tate had his bedroll laid out, and Shady picketed, the gray light of morning was just beginning to show, and he felt comfortable with a small fire of dried cottonwood, just enough to make some coffee and hang some strips of smoked meat for a warm meal before turning in to his blankets. Lobo had stretched out beside him, caught the few scraps thrown, and was soon asleep. Tate stretched out, hands behind his head as he began to pray and think what he must do to determine what the Crow war party might be planning. He had no idea what it was going to take, but he was determined to do whatever was necessary to make the area safe for his family.

He was restless but didn't want to move until at least twilight. After the coffee when they first stopped, he kept a cold camp through the day to prevent any smell of smoke that would be easily detected. He was stretched out on his bedroll, still trying to formulate a plan when Lobo came quickly to his feet and Shady turned with ears pricked as he looked down the draw. Tate came to one knee, looked but could see nothing with the brush and cottonwood obscuring his view. But he heard hoofbeats, several of them.

He picked up his bow and quiver and followed Lobo through the brush closer to the mouth of the draw. Lobo stopped and lowered his head, his lip curled in a snarl and eyes squinted. His body leaned forward, but his feet stayed in place, the stance was one of attack and Tate recognized the sign of danger. Tate dropped to one knee and slowly pushed aside the branches of the thick oak brush. Across the river, moving along the trail below the alkali covered ridge, rode several Crow. He counted at least twenty, enough for a raiding party or a hunting party, but not as many as had hit the wagon train.

As he watched, he also saw they were leading some additional horses, probably to pack meat. So, this was a hunting party, maybe. Those extra horses could also be used to pack plunder and captives. It was unusual for a hunting party to leave camp in the evening, hunts always started in the early morning, but if they had to travel, perhaps. He knew the buffalo herds were still to the south, unusual for this time of year, but if they were bound for the buffalo, well...his gut was telling him this was not just a hunting party. He looked down at Lobo, stroked the fur at his neck and whispered, "Good boy, yeah, we'll follow 'em. I'm thinkin' they're up to no good so we'll just see." He lifted his eyes to the sky, calculated about a half hours light was left, then turned back to his camp to get ready for his night's journey.

CHAPTER NINE
PURSUIT

THE SUMMER MIGRATION OF BUFFALO BROUGHT THE WOOLY beasts north from the southern grasslands would often come in waves with massive herds churning the ground with their passing and consuming everything green in their path. Some herds would travel across the Laramie River basin and on to the grasslands north of the Platte River. Some would come from the southwestern grasslands, travel across the great basin toward the Sweetwater River and on to the valley of the Wind River. The Owl Creek Mountains on the east and the Wind River Mountains on the west served as a natural funnel to bring the buffalo to hunting grounds of the Crow and Arapaho and other Indian tribes. Although, this year saw fewer buffalo, smaller herds and few crossing the Sweetwater into the more northern valleys, making the hunters desperate for game.

Tate wanted this party of Crow to be a hunting party and concerned only with gaining meat for their people, but his gut told him differently. The passing of the band of Crow was in the twilight of the day, now darkness covered the land and Tate mounted up to follow. It was an easy trail, they followed an established route downriver beside the Wind, turned west along the Popo Agie and crossed over to follow the Beaver. Their direction was generally south and once along the Beaver, Tate expected to find their camp. He estimated they would have made the Beaver right at dark and would have no reason to travel any further in the darkness.

He crossed the Popo Agie and as Shady mounted the low bank, he paused, letting the horse shake free of the water, and Tate stepped down to examine the tracks before him. Lobo sat on his haunches, watching the man, waiting. Tate knew the area, having hunted here before. With the confluence of three streams, the nearby flats were green and inviting to all manner of game and had always been a good hunting area. The dim light of night showed many shadows, but Tate was looking for a definite indication of the Crow camp.

As he brought up the memory of the area, he recalled the long ridge to the east of the river, separated from the valley of the Beaver by a stretch of alkali laden finger ridges and draws. With the Beaver being a meandering river that had carved its way across the flats, the greenery in the bottom of the valley drew its sustenance from the boggy banks and sandy soil. There were willows, alders, and a few stunted cottonwoods, but nothing of size that would provide cover.

He looked to the wolf, "Lobo, I think we'll swing wide o' them fellers and get ahead of 'em, maybe figger out what they're gonna do 'fore they do it." He stepped back aboard Shady and motioned Lobo to stay near as he turned away from the river bottom and started toward the long ridge on the east. He had gone no more than a quarter mile when he saw the twinkling of campfires on a cutback point of the Beaver. As he had guessed, the Crow made camp by the river and were having their evening meal.

Tate kept below the top of the ridge as he continued south, working his way around the camping Crow and staying at least a half mile from the trail they followed. Their course was taking them due south, and Tate knew where they were headed. Beyond the area known as Sand Draw, was a good location for buffalo, but also the Oregon Trail followed the Sweetwater River west before turning northwest to South Pass. And he knew the perfect place where he could glass the entire area and watch their progress.

It was well after midnight when Tate pointed Shady toward the crest of the high ridge before them. As they mounted the draw, they stopped at a small spring that Tate remembered as Wagon Bed Spring, named after some stubborn minded pilgrim who separated himself from a wagon train, thinking he could find his own way and found a way into the middle of a waiting war party. There was still the hub of a wheel nearby that marked the place and Tate stepped down to give Shady a bit of respite and to refill his canteen.

A short while later, they crested the promontory over-looking all of Sand Draw and the flats beyond. He pick-eted Shady near a couple of junipers and some bunch grass, walked to the edge of the ridge and found a good spot to stretch out his bedroll and with his floppy hat over his eyes, he drifted off to sleep, knowing the rising sun would wake him, probably bathing his face in bright sunshine before the light drove the shadows from the draws below.

Gray light painted the sky and peeked under the floppy brim of Tate's hat to bring the man wide awake. He slowly slipped the lid from his face, looked around without moving, and sat up to greet the morning. His rifle and brass telescope were at his side and he swiveled around on his rump to lift his glass to scan the valley beyond. His first cursory once-over revealed nothing of interest and he went to his parfleche to dig out some vittles. He went to the scattered juniper where Shady was tethered and gathered some long-dried sticks to make a smokeless fire, but he built it near the tree, so the over-hanging branches would filter whatever smoke there might be, leaving nothing to give away his campsite.

He fried some thin slices of smoked elk meat, split a biscuit and laid it over the meat to warm it up, and poured himself a cup of java to round out his breakfast. Once he had his fill and shared the bounty with Lobo, he went to his blankets at the edge of the ridge and bellied down to do some serious searching of the distant flats. With his elbows to stabilize the scope, he slowly scanned the green draw that held Beaver Creek, searching for the Crow party. When he finally spotted movement, he saw the group had scattered, obviously searching for game. They covered the entire creek bottom and a couple were wider out in the dry flats. Tate searched the valley before them, and spotted a small bunch of buffalo, lazily grazing on the outside of a wide bend of the creek. There were only five of six buffalo, but if they took them all, it would be a good load to carry back to their village.

He turned back toward the valley of the Sweetwater and began to scan the length of the stream. The Sweetwater and the Oregon Trail paralleled one another through a prairie flats bounded by the low rising and rocky Granite Mountains on the north edge. Tate's point on the top of the far ridge overlooked those mountains and gave a panoramic view of the Sweetwater bottom. He moved his scope the length of the Sweetwater, scanning the green bottom land and the wagon trail beyond. Although there were a few spots hidden behind the taller rocky-topped hills, what he saw revealed no movement, at least of anything bigger than an antelope.

He rolled back onto his stomach and stretched out to watch the valley of the Beaver. The headwaters of the river were just south of South Pass, there it had an intermittent flow dependent on the rainfall or late season snowmelt. By most standards it would be called no more than a creek with a width at most of ten yards and a regular flow of no greater than a couple of feet in depth. But in a desolate barren land, water brought life and drew game.

As Tate watched, the Crow had spotted the buffalo and were starting their stalk. Within moments, several mounted hunters charged at the beasts, driving them toward others that lay in wait, but Tate was surprised to see they only dropped three of the buffalo and the others made a running escape. He scowled in thought as he watched the warriors begin the work usually done by women, butchering the kills. Each of the downed buffalo was tended by four warriors while the remainder of the hunting party gathered by the horses near the creek. He was too far away to make out any differences among the warriors, but when two men mounted and started away at a canter, he looked back to see one prominent figure standing with arms crossed and watching them leave. That man had a pompadour top knot with feathers dangling to the side, his long hair hanging in braids over his shoulders. He wore a vest, breechcloth and leggings and was obviously in command of the group.

Tate swung his scope to follow the two that left and watched as they turned from the valley of the Beaver and started directly south. They could only be bound toward the Sweetwater to scout out the wagon trail by the river. He twisted around to scope the trail behind him and even before he brought the scope to his eye he saw a rising cloud of dust. He sat up, bringing his knees up to rest his elbows, and brought the scope to his eye to search the valley and the wagon trail. Wagons! He counted at least a dozen, maybe more, and they would soon be within view of the scouts and would probably be in danger of attack.

Tate's back was to the sun as he turned to find the scouts. He watched as they came to the Granite Mountains, dismounted and climbed quickly to the crest to look into the valley. Within moments, they spotted what they searched for and quickly ran back to their horses, reined around and started to the hunting party at a canter.

Tate had a pretty good idea what would happen and quickly packed up his gear. He watched as the scouts returned to the hunters and reported. The big man with the topknot started barking orders and waving his arms as his men responded. It was obvious he was assigning the task of finishing the butchering and packing the buffalo to a few men to be left behind or to return to their village.

The others were mounting up and Tate knew they would be coming for the wagons.

He slipped the scope into his saddle bags and swung aboard Shady. He knew he could get to the wagons before the Crow, but the pilgrims would need time to mount a defense. Their lives were in danger and the readying of the people might not happen if he didn't get there with his warning in time. He dug his heels into Shady's ribs and they started to the wagon trail at a canter, Lobo leading the way.

CHAPTER TEN
PREPARATIONS

H̲E̲ ̲G̲U̲E̲S̲S̲E̲D̲ ̲T̲H̲E̲ ̲D̲I̲S̲T̲A̲N̲C̲E̲ ̲T̲O̲ ̲T̲H̲E̲ ̲W̲A̲G̲O̲N̲S̲ ̲T̲O̲ ̲B̲E̲ ̲F̲O̲U̲R̲ ̲O̲R̲ five miles, but the country was rough with draws, dry creek beds, ravines, ridges and rocks. He slowed the pace of Shady, picking his way through the basaltic rock and scattered juniper and cedar. He rode a narrow ridge that would take him to a broad shoulder that sloped to the Sweetwater Creek bottom. Once at the creek bank, he gigged Shady across the shallow stream and up the far bank. He spotted the wagons, winding their way along the dusty road, mule teams shuffling in the loose sandy soil. The hardest pull for a team was through loose soil, but mules would stubbornly dig deep and pull the load far better than oxen or horses. Tate stood in his stirrups and turned to look back the way he came, searching for any sign of the Crow.

Tate gigged Shady to a trot toward the lead wagon and the two men riding alongside. One man had a hand uplifted to stop the visitor and moved ahead of the wagon to stop in front of Tate. The second man held his rifle across the pommel and pointed in Tate's direction. Tate smiled and nodded toward the rifle, "You're gonna need that, but not for me. I've come to warn you about a Crow war party headin' your way." He watched the men for their reaction, knowing it would give him a good idea as to what kind of men he faced, wondering if they would accept his warning.

The man without the rifle leaned forward, both hands on the saddle horn and said, "And you know that how?"

The man's skepticism was understandable, but unwarranted. Tate turned to face the questioner, "I've been followin' 'em for a spell, I think they're the same ones that wiped out a wagon train 'bout a week ago up on South Pass. I figger you got 'bout an hour before they're here."

"How many?"

"Couple dozen."

"You appear to be a bit experienced with these Indians, any suggestions?"

"Yeah, get ready. You got enough men to put up a fight?" asked Tate, looking to the man with the rifle and standing in his stirrups to look to the wagons. He wasn't impressed. None of the people showed concern, nor friendliness. Curiosity maybe, but not alarm. Tate didn't see any rifles at the ready, just the usual peaceful settlers more intent on getting to the land of promise. They were typical of the tired travelers, coming from a civilized land with law and order and the only danger was that of missing the dinner chime. Tate shook his head at the innocence and willful ignorance.

Tate had identified the two men as the wagonmaster and scout and listened as they explained. "We've got the usual group o' folks, all of 'em got rifles and such, but ain't none of 'em experienced fighters."

"They're about to get more experience than they want."

"So, you really think we're in that much danger?"

"Ummhumm, and unless you get ready, they're gonna be down on you and your scalps will be decorating some bucs lance!"

"Then we better get the wagons circled up. By the way, my name's Morgan, yours?"

"Tate."

Morgan turned to his partner, "Smitty, you ride back 'bout half way and start passin' the word. Tell 'em to get circled up quick and unhitched. Put the animals in the middle and get their rifles ready! Go on now!" He turned back to the closest wagon, stood in his stirrups and made a circling motion with his hand overhead and shouted, "Circle up! Now! Injuns comin'!"

Lobo dropped to his belly beside Shady as Tate leaned on his pommel and watched the activity. Morgan was apparently the wagon master and he rode back along the wagons and hollered instructions to each driver. As Tate watched, he spoke aloud but softly, as was his custom when the only listeners were Shady and Lobo, "Well, if nothin' else, these folks know how to handle them mules and get the wagons circled. Guess we better get inside the circle an' see if we can help a mite." He looked down to Lobo and said, "You stay close, boy. Don't wanna go scarin' all these womenfolk."

He tethered Shady to the big back wheel of a wagon that held a couple of towheaded youngsters that were watching all the activity from within the wagon, their heads sticking out from under the canvas bonnet. The older boy watched Tate tie Shady off and asked, "Are you a mountain man?" Tate chuckled and saw the boy looking at his buckskins and then down to Lobo. "Is that a wolf?" he asked, wide eyed.

"Yes, and yes. You could say I'm a mountain man, and that is a wolf. His name is Lobo, but don't go near him unless I'm around, alright?"

"Sure mister. Are there Injuns comin'?"

"There are, so you and your sister there be sure to keep down in the wagon when everything starts, understand?"

"Ummmhummm. We will."

Tate saw the wagonmaster coming his way and he turned to meet him. Three other men were following close behind, one with a frock coat and a string tie, appeared to be a minister carrying a Bible in hand and a stern look on his face. As they neared, the minister stepped forward, "Why do you think these Indians will attack us? Shouldn't we try to talk to them first?" He shook his Bible for emphasis and Tate scowled at the man, shaking his head at his ignorance.

Before he could answer, another of the followers asked in a high pitched and somewhat whiney voice, "Why would they want to attack us anyway. We haven't done anything to them?"

Tate looked to Morgan, saw the man drop his eyes and shake his head and wait for Tate to answer. "Well, first let me ask you, why do you think the Indians won't attack you?"

"Why, we haven't done anything to them, so why should they?"

"Humm, well, why should they? Do you have anything they might want?" asked Tate, seriously.

"Uh, uh, what?" asked the whiney voiced milquetoast.

"Well, let me see. They want your rifles, your food, your animals, your women and your children, and anything else that takes their fancy!"

The man gasped and stepped back, hand to his mouth. The minister asked again, "Well, why can't we talk to them first. We shouldn't just start shooting. They are God's children too!" he declared, patting his worn leather Bible to emphasize what he perceived as the foundation of his belief.

"Parson, do you speak Crow? And even if you did, what would you say? Would you offer them this man's wife and children to leave the rest of you alone?"

"Well, uh, I uh, . . . "

Before he could say more, Tate, obviously losing his patience, "Look people. I just picked up after another one of these attacks about a week ago and not too far from here. That train had fewer wagons, but I had to pick up broken, bloody, burned and mutilated bodies of about thirty pilgrims just like you. Everyone of 'em just as well-meaning as you, and everyone of 'em dead, just like you're gonna be if you don't get ready. It's gonna be kill or be killed! Do you understand that!" he was standing and shouting at the end of his comments, driving everyone back away from him.

The wagonmaster looked up and said, "Thanks! They needed that. That minister, if he really is one, has been the most parsimonious blood-sucking leech and whenever anyone resists his plea for help he starts preachin' an' won't let up til they give him whatever he wants. When he joined up, the folks were glad to have a preacher, but the only thing he brought with him was his Bible an' his attitude. Now, you mentioned tradin', do you think they'd take him in trade?"

Tate chuckled at the suggestion and said, "I think the Crow are already mad enough as it is, we don't need to stir 'em up anymore."

"How 'boutchu comin' along and help me check on ever'body, see if we can help 'em get set?" asked Morgan, starting out to walk the circle.

As they checked each wagon, Tate was introduced and welcomed, and he made a few suggestions. He looked at each of the weapons, noted a few had Hawkens, others had percussion cap or flintlock Kentucky style rifles, and only one old-timer sported a new Sharps. When Tate saw the man with the Sharps, he asked, "Shoot that thing much?"

"Only when I needs to," answered the man simply, showing an almost toothless grin.

"Can you hit anything?"

"Onliest time I ever missed, was when I was a younker and the rifle was bigger'n me."

Tate grinned at the man, noted his wagon and looked to the wagonmaster, "Anybody else have a Sharps?"

Morgan shook his head and grinned, "Just me. But I can tell you're thinkin' somethin', what is it?"

Tate stepped up on the hub of a wheel of the nearby wagon, up to the seat and stood in the seat to look to the creek bottom about a hundred yards away. He shaded his eyes and scanned the creek bank and dropped back beside the wagonmaster.

"Here's what I'm thinkin'. There's three of us with Sharps and I don't think these Crow have been properly introduced to Mr. Sharps, an' I reckon we oughta do that.

Now, you see that dip in the creek bank yonder," he pointed to the low cut about two hundred yards upstream. Morgan looked where Tate pointed, and listened as the man of the mountains began to outline his plan. Morgan sent one of the other men to fetch the old-timer that he called Charley and turned back to listen to Tate. As he spoke, Tate was thinking and looking all the while. He took a deep breath and let it out slowly, "So, whaddaya think?"

"Should work. I'm willin' to try anything if it'll save our skin," answered the wagonmaster and looked to see Charley coming. "I'll fill Charley in on it an' we'll get in position. If what you were thinkin' is right, they should be along just any minute now."

MANY OF THE SETTLERS WERE STILL FRANTICALLY STACKING boxes, arranging trunks, anything that would provide cover while others made a secondary line of protection for the children. Most of the women had stationed themselves so they could readily reload for the men, but others, confident of their own marksmanship, found a place that would enable them to use their rifles or shotguns. Tate was on the lookout, scanning the far hillsides and ravines for the raiding party, ready to sound the alarm and put their plan into action. He watched a bit of a dust cloud and soon saw the Crow crest the slight knoll above the river. Tate sounded the alarm, "Look lively, here they come!"

The Crow leaders reined up to survey their target, able to scan the valley from the rise on the far side of the river. The man Tate had supposed to be their leader was motioning and directing his warriors, readying for the attack. Tate turned back to Morgan and said, "Just like we figgered!" Tate stepped down from the wagon seat and took up his Sharps and hollered to Morgan who was headed to his position, "I'll take the first shot." Morgan nodded and quickly stepped to his chosen place for the defense.

Where the leaders of the Crow were sitting on their horses was across the river and about five hundred yards from the wagons, what would normally be out of range of the white men's rifles. Tate knew the usual tactic of the Indians was to send in a first wave of attackers to draw the fire, and before the defenders could reload, the second wave of attackers, usually larger, would go against their quarry, believing them to be defenseless. And Tate watched as the first group, of eight or ten warriors started across the shallow stream to attack. Tate's plan was to let the first wave attack, and as the second started, he and the other two with Sharps would fire on the leaders who thought themselves out of range.

But as the first group came from the river, a white man in a black frock coat, jumped from the brush before them, hands raised and started shouting to the Indians. Tate immediately recognized him as the minister. Although Tate could not hear what he was saying, he watched as the man waved the Bible with one hand and shouted to the Indians as loud as he could. The Crow, who started to kick their horses to a gallop to attack, reined up, showing their shock at seeing this man, unarmed and screaming at them. Tate realized that the Crow probably didn't understand English and perhaps thought the man's screaming was either his war cry or his death song and they nodded to one another and charged at the crazy white man.

Tate swung his rifle towards the charging Indians and

fired at the one nearest to the minister, knocking him from his horse, but the others didn't slow and within seconds, the minister was riddled with arrows and the last warrior thrust his lance into the man's body as he passed. Tate quickly reloaded and turned back to take aim at the leaders, but the others, thinking Tate's first shot was their signal to start had already taken their shots at the leaders and when Tate looked back to the hillside, all he saw was the disappearing back of one of the warriors, and two rider-less horses following. The bodies of two attackers lay splayed on the slope, and Tate turned his attention back to the Indians attacking the wagons.

The big boom of his Sharps joined the raucous cacophony of the attack. War cries of the Indians, screams of the women of the wagons, rifle fire, and braying mules seemed to echo back from the hillsides and what seemed to last for hours was just a few minutes. When the second wave of attackers came, they soon realized their leaders had fled and the rest of the Crow soon followed in their retreat across the river. When the people of the wagons saw the Indians take flight, several stood and cheered and laughed, relieving the tension, but soon turned to take tally of damage done and fellow pilgrims that might be wounded or killed.

Morgan, grinning widely and came to Tate, hand outstretched, "Tate, we did it! Just like you figgered!" Tate looked at the man and answered, "Well, I'm sorry I shot too soon, but that crazy minister . . . "

Morgan dropped his eyes to the ground and looked up with a somber expression, "Yeah, who'd ever thought he'da done sumthin' like that! After travelin' with that man, all he ever did was make a nuisance of himself an' ever'body was thinkin' he was a phony, but guess he really believed what he was spoutin'."

"You never can tell about folks. Sometimes they talk a lot about sum'thin', tryin' to convince others when the one they're really tryin' to convince is themselves. Now, when it comes to what the Bible teaches, I'm a firm believer that everything in that book is God's word. But sometimes, well-meaning though they may be, some folks just try to complicate what is really quite simple. You know, he didn't have to die for what he wanted to believe, Jesus already did that for us. All we have to do is accept what Christ did for us and receive that gift of eternal life. Course, He does want us to tell others about it, but not like he was wanting to do."

The wagonmaster looked at Tate with a sideways glance, wondering about this man that came out of nowhere to warn them and save them from what could have been a massacre. Morgan shook his head and said, "That's the last thing I expected to hear from you. But you're right, that's exactly what my momma told me all the days of my childhood and I couldn't wait to get away from it, but hearin' it from you, maybe she was right."

Tate grinned at the man, "I didn't know your momma, but I'm sure she was right if what she taught you was what I just said. Better think on it and do somethin' about it. You might not get a warning before your next Indian attack!"

"Hehehe, yessiree, ain't had that much fun in a long while!" declared Charley as he walked bow-legged up to the two men. "Now, one o' us missed, an' I know it weren't me, so which one you two younkers was it?"

Tate chuckled at the old-timer standing before them

and leaning on the muzzle of his Sharps. He looked every bit the part of an old mountain man, greased darkened buckskins, long scraggly gray hair protruding from under his floppy felt hat that sported a feather and grinning with an almost toothless smile as he cackled.

"I'm afraid it was me, old-timer. By the time I was ready to squeeze it off, that top-knot wearing Crow was disappearin' over the edge of that hill," answered Tate.

"Well, in his defense, he dropped the first Indian that was goin' after that crazy Bible-Thumper," responded Morgan.

"So, what're ye gonna do now?" asked the old man with his gravelly voice as he scowled at Tate from under his gray eyebrows that resembled sage brush in the winter.

"I'm goin' after 'em."

"You're goin' after 'em? What on earth fer? You anxious to lose yore top-knot?" asked the old man.

"No, but I'm thinkin' that one I missed is the same leader that hit that other wagon train, and probably some o' the other attacks that have been happenin', and he needs to be stopped."

The old man looked around, back to Tate and said, "From what I recomember 'bout Injuns, after a leader gets whupped like he just done, he ain't likely to get too many followers next time."

"You're right about that, but there's always young bucs that'll follow anybody and this one's had some raids where his warriors got lots of plunder an' honors, so he'll probably get more. But even if he don't, I'm thinkin' he'd probably turn renegade and get some to follow him. Either way, he needs to be stopped," explained Tate.

"You need some h'ep?" asked the old-timer hopefully.

Tate considered the offer, thought better of it and answered, "I tell you how you could help, if you're game."

"Name it!"

"You folks are goin' o'er South Pass, right?" asked Tate, looking to Morgan, who nodded, "and that's not too far from my cabin. I've got a wife and some youn'uns there, an' if you'd look in on 'em, I'd appreciate it. Cuz, if I foller these Crow very far, it might be a while 'fore I get back there myself."

The old-timer grinned, "I can do that, sure'nuff."

Tate looked to the wagonmaster and said, "Would you happen to have some folks here that'd like to have a couple young'uns, do ya?"

Morgan frowned and asked, "Uh, you tryin' to unload yours?"

Tate scowled and then laughed, "Oh, no, not that. But that other wagon train I told you about, well, there was a couple, a boy and a girl, both about fifteen, that escaped from that massacre and they don't have any family left. They were bound for Oregon, I think, but they don't have any family there either. I thought if you had somebody wanting to take 'em under wing, well, maybe . . . " he shrugged his shoulders and looked hopefully to the wagonmaster, who was grinning.

"We might, I know there's a family that lost their only child in an accident a couple years back, that's why they're headin' west with us, to have a fresh start and to get away from where it happened. I'll talk to 'em."

"But first, I suggest you get the wagons movin'. I don't think them Crow will be attackin' again, but they might wanna come get their dead. So, it'd be a good thing to be gone when they do, don' you think?" suggested Tate.

"You're right," answered Morgan and began passing the word to get ready to move out. Tate volunteered to fetch the body of the minister but also suggested they take him with them and bury him wherever they stop. Morgan agreed, and the wagons were on the move. Tate watched as they moved out, turned to mount up, and with Lobo leading the way, started back towards Sand Draw and his lookout to track down the raiding party.

TATE CHOSE TO TAKE A CIRCUITOUS ROUTE AWAY FROM THE site of the wagon attack. With the possibility of the raiding party returning for their dead, he did not want to risk the Crow catching sight of him. He moved back eastward along the wagon trail, using the churned soil from the wagons and the mule teams to mask the tracks of Shady and traveled a couple of miles. When the trail came near the Sweetwater he turned to cross the shallow waters and take up his vigil from the rocky hills that bordered the river.

The Sweetwater ran straight and narrow as it passed a yellow-walled adobe hillside with narrow run-off ravines, then made a dog-leg turn to the south and then back east. It was on a ridge overlooking this stretch of the Sweetwater that Tate bellied down and used his scope to watch the battleground for the return of the raiding party. Tate knew that if a leader of a war party had suffered a defeat, the shame was bad enough, but to fail to return without the bodies of the dead would be unforgiveable. If the dead were not given the proper respect and their families allowed to mourn, the responsible leader could be ostracized and banished from the tribe.

Tate turned back to look at Shady grazing in the shade of the ponderosa, in the bottom of the draw. Lobo was stretched out nearby, enjoying the respite from the hot sun. It was early afternoon and Tate hoped his wait would not be long, laying on the sun-baked hillside was far from comfortable. And he didn't have long to wait. He had no sooner picked up the scope, when he saw the war party filing from the stream crossing and leading the ponies of the fallen warriors toward the battleground. He watched as they draped the bodies over the horses, secured them and were soon starting back to cross the stream, taking the same course to the north. Tate rolled over, sat up and decided to wait until dark to resume his chase. He slid down the gravelly slope to the bottom of the grassy draw and went to retrieve his parfleche and prepare some coffee and vittles. After rubbing down Shady with a handful of dry grass, he gathered some dry wood for a fire. He was hungry and tired, and thinking that a few hours of good rest would be welcome.

AN OVERZEALOUS RED fox chasing a scampering rabbit jumped over the outstretched legs of Tate and brought the man instantly awake. Dusk had already given way to the blue-black of a star-sprinkled night and the full moon winked from behind a shadowy cloud when Tate sat up. He looked to Shady, who stood watching his friend with curious eyes, and Lobo, who sat on his haunches, red tongue lolling to the side of his smiling face. Both waited patiently for the man that would get them back on the trail of the marauding Indians. Tate slid off his blanket and rolled the bedroll. Once Shady was saddled, bags tied on and the bedroll secured behind the cantle, Tate tied on the parfleche, checked the scabbard with the rifle, the sheath with the Longbow, hung the quiver beside the saddle bags, and swung aboard to start the chase.

He followed the stream bed of Long Creek to the northwest, knowing he could go from the headwaters of the creek, cross Sand Draw and come to Beaver Creek and hopefully pick up the trail of the Crow somewhere near the location of their campsite of the previous night. The eastern sky was still dark, and Tate guessed it to be maybe four hours past midnight when the saw the winding Beaver Creek before him. He reined up beside a large boulder at the foot of a hillock, climbed atop and scanned the dark line of the creek. After several moments of searching, he finally saw a thin trail of smoke from a dying fire, but he wasn't sure if it was the war party. He returned to retrieve his scope, thinking he might have to wait until there was a little light to be certain.

He had just gotten comfortable when the first hint of light marked the eastern horizon, and Tate lifted his telescope to search what he believed was the campsite of the Crow. He saw movement, and spotted the string of horses, most standing three-legged and drowsing, but a couple were busy swatting at deer flies with their tails. He was about two hundred fifty yards from their camp and amidst a cluster of juniper. He looked around, seeing several more junipers, some cedar and pinyon, a few ponderosa and a lot of boulders that marked the hillside beside and behind him. He grinned as he formed his plan.

Tate quickly retrieved and strung his longbow, started back up the hillside as he nocked an arrow, and turned to take aim. He breathed deep, stepped into, or as the English put it, lay his body into his bow, bringing the black obsidian tipped arrow to full draw, elevated it just a bit, and let the arrow fly. He watched the flight as far as he could see it, but as it disappeared in the dim light he went to Shady, mounted up and trotted through the trees and well away from the hillside and toward the confluence of the Wind and Popo Agie rivers. He was below a low rise and knew he was out of sight of the Indians, and smirked as he imagined the reaction of the war party when the arrow found its target. Tate wasn't concerned with who or what it hit, he just wanted the leader of the warriors to know they were seen and someone was making them the prey instead of the predator.

HAD Tate been within rock-throwing distance of the camp of the Crow, he could not have made a better shot nor picked a better target than the one his randomly shot arrow found. There were two or three of the warriors moving from their blankets, one stirring up the fire, another starting for the bushes by the stream, when the long black arrow whispered through the night and impaled itself between the legs and through the blanket of Bad Heart Bear. The muted thunk and the movement of his blanket brought Bear instantly awake and when he saw the arrow between his knees, he shouted "Aiiieeee!" and jumped to his feet, knife in one hand and tomahawk in the other as he searched the tree-line for an attacker.

His shout startled the others awake and blankets flew,

warriors sprang to their feet, weapons were snatched up and men scattered in all directions. When there was no immediate threat seen, the men walked back to their blankets as they heard Bear shout, "Who did this?! Where is he that shot this arrow!" Most stared at the arrow stuck in the blanket, pinning the blanket to the ground, unable to answer their leader's question. Bear motioned to the arrow, shouted, "Who?!"

Everyone looked around, several with bows in hand, waiting for an attack. But only Spotted Horse came near. He looked at the arrow, looked back along the angle of the shaft, and walked to the edge of the trees to scan the flats beyond. He turned back to Bear, shrugged his shoulders, "I see no one! The land is flat, there is no one! Whoever shot that arrow has fled, hidden, gone."

"You! And you!" Bear motioned first to Spotted Horse and then to Crazy Fox, "Go, find the sign, tell me where he is!"

The two men scurried to their mounts, taking off at a canter, leaning down to search the ground for tracks, to try to find the shooter of the arrow. When they left, Bear turned to the others and directed them to get ready to follow. His anger was evident as he barked his orders, threatening with his motions and his tone. The arrow was a challenge, an insult, a warning, and he wanted whoever dared to threaten him to be caught, tortured, and killed. With the shame of the defeat upon him, the thought of anyone threatening him was more than he could handle, and he had to wash away that humiliation with the blood of his taunting enemy.

The entire war party followed their leader as he rode to where the others were still searching for any sign of the lone attacker. When Bear rode up to Crazy Fox, the man said, "There is nothing! No tracks, no sign. This is too far from our camp for an arrow, we searched everything from the trees to here. No arrow can fly that far and there is no sign!"

"Ha! You are blind! You!" he motioned to Spotted Horse, "Are you also blind? Where is this man that dares to shoot into our camp?!"

Spotted Horse also shrugged his shoulders, looked down to the ground, and said, "There are no tracks. Perhaps it is a spirit?"

The mention of a spirit caused the others to look from one to another, and then to Bear. He held up the black arrow, and waved it in the air, "This is no spirit! It is an arrow!"

But the sight of a black arrow, that was longer than most, with a black point, black feather, but only two thin white rings around the shaft, was like no other they had ever seen. As they looked at the arrow, the words of Spotted Horse resonated with the warriors and they spoke quietly with one another. Their mumbling angered Bear and he screamed, "Find him!" and gigged his horse back toward the trail by Beaver Creek.

The others milled about, searching for tracks, but they all knew any possible tracks had been obliterated by the many warriors in their group. Spotted Horse told Crazy Fox, "You, scout ahead, look for tracks. We will go with Bear."

BAD HEART BEAR SAT WITH A STOIC EXPRESSION AS HE
listened to Rotten Tail, the medicine man of the people.
Rotten Tail addressed the council of elders and chiefs and
Blood Woman and Red Bear, seated in the place of honor
amidst the elders listened to the Shaman as he told of
Bear's recent move against the wagons of the whites. It
was well known that several of the leaders were not
happy with Bad Heart Bear taking the name of one of
their ancients who led their people to this country,
Daasítchileetash, or Bear Whose Heart is Never Good.

Rotten Tail began, "When Bad Heart Bear led our
warriors against the wagons on the trail that crosses the
Winds, they returned with many goods and our warriors
earned honors from the scalps taken and the battle won.
Now he has taken many against more of the whites and
returned only with the bodies of five of our warriors and
no goods or scalps. We must question if this is true
Xapáaliia, from the Creator, or if he goes in his own

strength and leads our warriors to their deaths. When our people go hungry, he does little to help our people."

The Shaman, with his headdress the cap of the skull of a buffalo, with the black fur and horns atop and the neck fur trailing behind, was an impressive and powerful man among the people and his judgement was never questioned, at least not aloud. He scowled at Bear, thinking him an impertinent and dangerous warrior that sought only his own glory, then turned back to the chiefs, "On his return, his warriors tell of a 'Spirit Arrow' that came into their camp. Perhaps it is a warning from Akbaatatdia, the Creator."

Bad Heart Bear sat between Buffalo Horn and Crazy Fox and had grown antsy as he listened to the Shaman speak against him. He started to rise but was stopped by the uplifted hand of Blood Woman, the chief, "When this council met last, we agreed to consider what action was to be taken and to meet together again. You chose to take our young warriors and go out before the council spoke. We warned against anyone taking action that could bring judgment upon our people, and now we hear the cries of wives and mothers as they weep for those who have crossed over, those who rode with you, is this not the judgment of Akbaatatdia, the Great Spirit?" The elders and others nodded, beating the ground with their rattles and fists.

When the chief was seated, Bear rose, "It is true that I led our young warriors from this village before the council met again. But we left to hunt for meat for our village, and we brought back the meat from three buffalo, all for our people. On our hunt, our scouts saw the wagons, and we agreed it was a sign. We wanted to bring more than meat for our people, we knew the wagons of the whites would carry other foods and prizes and weapons for our people. That is why we attacked, it was for our people."

Iron Bull, a respected war leader and sub-chief, spoke, "But you did not take the wagons, you lost warriors, so this must have been against the Great Spirit!" Several nodded their agreement but quieted to hear Bear speak again.

"These white men had shoots-far-guns! Never before have we known of guns that can shoot two times," and he thrust forward two fingers, "as far as others. While we waited beyond the stream and on a mountain slope, more than four bow-shots from the wagons, their shoots-far-guns took the lives of those beside me! They shoot far and with a big noise!" Most of those within the lodge had not heard of these guns before and were wide-eyed at the report.

Iron Bull spoke again, "What of this 'Spirit Arrow'?"

Bear took a deep breath and reached down beside Crazy Fox, lifted the black shaft before him and said, "This is the arrow! It is but an arrow. We looked for the distance of two bow-shots and found no tracks, no sign. Where the arrow came from, I do not know. But if it is a Spirit Arrow as Rotten Tail believes, I would believe it is a good sign, that the Great Spirit is with us and will be with us when we go against these same wagons!"

"You would go against them again?" asked Iron Bull.

"Yes. When we attacked before, there was no cover and their shoots-far-guns could take us, but with more warriors and if we attack where their guns would not help them, we can take them and all the prizes, weapons, women, and goods!" Bear spoke loudly and roused the warriors around the circle. They shouted and beat the ground in agreement. He grinned widely and sat down to wait for the shouting to subside and for the leaders to speak.

When Bad Heart Bear left before the council reconvened in his absence, they had agreed to take the fight to the whites and others that stood with them. But Bear had acted rashly, and they wanted to show their authority by chastising or banishing him upon his return. But his story of a hunting party that brought back meat for the people and only took the wagons as a target of opportunity, gave them an out and now looked to one another for an agreement.

Blood Woman took the lead and looked to Rotten Tail and Iron Bull, then to Red Bear and Bull Chief, then to the white-haired elders on the far side of the circle. Seeing no opposition, he nodded to Bad Heart Bear, "You, Pretty Eagle, Spotted Horse, and Crazy Fox will take more warriors and take the wagons and any others that are the enemy of the people! If you are victorious, we will continue to fight against our enemies!" War cries burst forth from all the crowd and they rose to leave the lodge of the chief. As they scattered among the camp, shouts lifted, and drums began to beat as an impromptu war dance was gathered and the men began to ready themselves for war.

The elders stayed behind with the chiefs and Blood Woman spoke to them, "It is because our people are hungry, and the buffalo have not come. If Bad Heart Bear can take the wagons and bring much food back, our people will have a good season of snows. But if he cannot, our young warriors will be done with war and we can still mount a hunt for the buffalo. When Bear brought meat from this hunt, that tells me there are more buffalo to the south and we can move our camp. But if we are at war, those that would hunt will be after honors and our people will go hungry."

The elders and chiefs looked to one another, spoke softly among themselves and as the talk lulled, Red Bear spoke, "We know if they do not take the wagons, we will lose many warriors and our people will not be as strong. But warriors that do not follow the wisdom of the council do not make us strong. We have lived many summers, and we have seen the young people learn in both ways, the hard way and the better way. Maybe the Great Spirit will let them learn the better way."

TATE HAD RETURNED to his place of vigil atop the lone knoll that stood as a guardian over the camp of the Crow. It was late, and the milky way marched across a black sky as if charting a course for the moon. But when the sound of drums began and the shouting and screaming of war cries rose from the village, Tate knew this was an ominous warning of what was to come. This was no longer about a band of renegade young bucs wanting to gain honors and take a few scalps; this was shaping up to be an all-out war and Tate knew before the gold leaves of fall painted the mountains, the Crow warriors would paint them red with the blood of vengeance. His thoughts turned to his family, and he knew he must see to their safety before he continued this scout for General Harney of Fort Laramie. But he looked back at the camp below and visually measured the distance to the center where all the dancing had begun. *Humm, looks to be 'bout two hundred fifty, mebbe three hundred yards.* He grinned to himself and slipped back down to retrieve his longbow and quiver.

He moved just below the crest of the clay hill. He lifted his eyes to the dark sky that had a few scattered grey-bottomed clouds and the moon hung at the edge of a sizeable one, giving the figure a halo of moonlight. He watched as the moon slowly moved behind the cloud, then turned toward the camp below. Torches gave light to the warriors that danced to the rhythmic beat of the big drum casting grotesque shadows on the buffalo hide lodges. Tate nocked an arrow, leaned into the bow and brought it to full draw. He lifted the tip of straight above the dancers and let the shaft fly into the night. He scampered back over the crest of hard clay and hunkered down. He had barely bellied down when the chants turned to screams and war cries, and the figures that danced before the fire scattered. The drums ceased, and shouts lifted as orders were given to the warriors to search the night for the one that lofted another Spirit Arrow!

Even without knowing exactly where the arrow struck, Tate knew by the reaction of the people he had accomplished precisely what he had wanted. He turned and worked his way down to Shady, cautiously retracing his steps from rock to rock and doing his best to leave no sign behind that anyone had been there. Within moments, Tate, Lobo, and Shady started away into the darkness, enroute to the cabin in the woods and a reunion with his family.

CHAPTER FOURTEEN
WARNING

HIS CHOSEN ROUTE TOOK HIM ALMOST DUE SOUTH AWAY from the alkali ridges and across the Wind River. He kicked Shady up to a canter, knowing the flats before him were actually atop a wide plateau and they would soon come to the drop away to the lower valley that held the Little Wind River. As they came to the edge, he reined up and dropped to the ground, and picking the trail by the diminishing moon and star light, he led Shady off the plateau and down a wide ravine to the bottom. Lobo had already taken the trail and waited below, pacing and searching the beginning of the flats. Once reunited, the trio started again to the south. Tate would walk Shady for a while and when his impatience took over, he would gig him up to a canter. With the increased pace, they covered the flats in good time.

He judged it to be near midnight when they left the promontory, and they had been on the trail about six hours as the sun stretched lances of pink and orange from below the eastern horizon. Tate approached the brushy bank of the Popo Agie river, saw Lobo waiting with a wet muzzle and wide eyes. He stepped down, led Shady to the water and slipped off the saddle, bags, and parfleche. He rubbed Shady down with some dry grass, watched him roll in it, and turned to fetch some firewood for a small fire to make some coffee.

A man does some of his best thinking on the back of a horse. There's just something about the easy rhythmic gait, the creak of the leather, and the fresh air of the mountains, that sets a mind to pondering problems, working out solutions, generally resolving life's issues. Part of that mood is the trust in the horse beneath him, the solitude, being at one with God's creation. But with each individual that seclusion takes the form that only that man needs. All the while Tate was traveling across the sage covered flats, the silhouette of the Wind River mountains before him and the cool air in his face, he was turning things over in his mind. He thought of his family, their home, their many friends, and the others that God always seemed to put in his path to help. He considered the Crow and what their next quarry might be, the wagons and if they were in danger from those same Crow, or the Arapaho as the enemy of the Crow and the attack that had taken many of their people. And as he considered, he began to put the pieces of the puzzle together.

His southward travel had taken him nearer the mountains and he had thought about the trail that would follow the Popo Agie into the Winds, knowing that would be a little shorter and would get him to the cabin sooner. His concern was for Shady; he had traveled far these last few days and to push on without at least a day's rest might be more than he could take. Then he remembered the words of Whiskers about the location of the Arapaho camp. He grinned to himself, tossed the dregs of the coffee from his cup and began saddling up to start up the Popo Agie.

The Popo Agie meandered from the shoulders of the granite peaks of the Wind River Mountains. The cascading water gurgleed over falls and through the rocky canyons and in the middle of the lower canyon, the stream disappeared underground and rose almost a mile lower. Called the Sinks by the early explorers and the Indians, it was also thought to be a place of mystery and power. Tate considered this as he passed the rise from the Sinks and followed the trail that twisted between. As the early morning sun warmed his back, he pushed Shady to follow the trail that angled up the rocky juniper covered slope to his right. With a cluster of aspen to mark the shoulder and the trail, they soon crested the flat of the shoulder and pushed into the trees. He heard the series of waterfalls thundering over the rocks in their search of the pools below, but they were small, and the flow of the water continued crashing white to the lower course.

Shortly after passing the falls, Tate crossed over the creek and pointed Shady to an aspen crowded draw the led up the slope to the flat above. He recognized the area and knew he was nearing a place called Deer park that would be the camp of the Arapaho. He also knew he was watched, he felt it since he cleared the falls and believed them to be scouts from the Arapaho camp. He caught a glimpse of the rump of a paint pony disappearing into the thicker timber before him, and he knew there were others beyond the aspen but staying hidden in the pines.

He reined up and peered through the pines to survey

the encampement. Bending to look beneath the branches
of an ancient ponderosa, he saw the village, most with
hide lodges, some with brush hut lodges, but a very busy
village. No alarm had been sounded, but two mounted
warriors were coming from the village on the trail he
followed. He continued forward, watching those before
him, feeling the others coming from beside and behind
him. The stoic expressions of the two that now held up
their hands to stop him told Tate he was not recognized.
He lifted his hand and greeted them in the language of the
Arapaho, "I come in peace. I am Longbow."

The scouts looked at the newcomer, and one of the
men began to smile, "You had a woman from our band as
your woman. I see you still have the wolf," he added,
motioning to Lobo with his lance.

Tate recognized his refusal to use the name of White
Fawn as the belief of the people. Like many of the native
people, it was their custom to not speak the names of
those that had died, believing it would cause their spirits
to be restless. Most believing that by using the name of
the departed, it would be the same as calling them back.

Tate grinned, "Yes, many summers ago, but my woman
has crossed over. I knew her brother who was your chief,
but I am told he too has crossed over. I would speak with
Red Pipe pieceas I have news for him."

"I am Broken Lance. Your woman was the daughter of
my mother's sister." Tate moved forward to greet the
warrior that was his cousin and clasped forearms with the
man. Lance motioned for him to follow as he said, "I will
take you to Red Pipe." He motioned to the others and they
moved away to return to their posts as watchers.

The word quickly spread through the camp and as the

two rode toward the central hide lodge several curious onlookers moved towards the riders, some greeting, most gawking. Tate wasn't uncomfortable among the Arapaho, but he definitely felt like a stranger or outsider. These were the people that made him and Kit Carson so welcome when they first met at the Green River rendezvous, but that was many years ago and even though there were probably still some that remembered, most saw him as a white man and intruder.

As they reined up before the lodge of Red Pipe the entry flap was pushed aside, and the chief came out, stood before his lodge and scowled at the visitor. Broken Lance greeted the chief and told of Longbow. The chief motioned for Tate to step down and with a motion summoned a young man to take the white man's horse. Red Pipe was an imposing figure with long braids interwoven with beaver fur, a scalp lock that held three dangling feathers, and a beaded buckskin vest that did little to hide his broad muscular chest. Heavy brows shadowed black eyes that hid any emotion and his large nose was slightly bent, probably from some battle. With a sweep of his hand he directed Tate to the log beside the fire circle that held glowing coals that kept a hanging pot warm.

"We will eat, then we will talk," tersely spoke the chief as he seated himself before a woven willow backrest.

His woman stepped from the lodge before the man was seated and carried two wooden platters as she moved to the pot. She quickly dished up the stew, handed the first platter to her man and the second to Tate, who nodded and spoke a word of thanks. The food was good, and Tate recognized it as elk meat with potatoes, onions, and squaw cabbage. With sizable platters, the helping was large and both men had their appetites sated with one serving.

When the woman had taken the empty plates, the chief began with, "The one you knew as chief was the son of my father's brother. He was a good leader, but the battle with the Crow took two hands of our warriors."

"That is why I have come to you. The Crow are taking the path of war. A war party took a wagon train on South Pass, killed everyone, six hands of whites were killed. They have also attacked several other camps of whites and another wagon train, on the trail by the Sweetwater."

"Is that not the work of a raiding party?"

"Well, it began as that, but I think the chiefs have let this war leader do more. I was by their camp last night an' they broke out the drums and started a big dance. That sounds to me like the whole camp is makin' war."

The chief slowly lifted his head and nodded as he considered. "Do you know where they will make this war?"

"I'm thinkin' they'll try for that wagon train again. They were surprised cuz the wagons were ready for 'em an' killed several of their warriors, but it also showed they had many rifles and stuff the Crow might be wantin', an' I'm thinkin' that little battle just made 'em mad. But from what I could tell, they were lookin' to the south from their camp by the small lake in the flats by the alkali ridge." Tate lifted his eyes from the chief to see the approach of the big man Whiskers, looking to Tate with the familiar grin that winked from behind the whiskers to show his tobacco stained teeth.

Tate stood to greet the man and was enveloped in a

bear hug by the man mountain. When he released Tate and stepped back, he asked, "What brings you to the camp?" His deep voice rumbled and reminded Tate of the sounds of the geysers he saw far to the north.

"Thought I'd give these folks a warnin' about the Crow bein' on the warpath, and to see if I could trade for another horse. I've got a long way to go and mine's plumb tuckered out."

"Well, I kin fix ya up with a horse, I've got a few I traded fer and ain't got no use fer."

The big man looked to the chief, and back to Tate, "You done with yer palaverin'?"

Tate looked to the chief and asked, "Is there any other way I can be of help to you?"

The chief stood, pulled his vest across his chest, and said, "We will talk again before you go. I will talk to my people and they may want to speak to you."

"Sure, sure." He turned to Whiskers and said, "Show me these horses," and the two started off together.

CHAPTER FIFTEEN
FREIGHTERS

THE WAGONS WERE TWO DAYS FROM THE SITE OF THEIR attack and had followed the Oregon Trail that paralleled the Sweetwater as the river made a wide bend to the southwest. Although the journey from Independence Rock and across the flats that followed the Sweetwater seemed to be just that, flat, it was a gradual climb. Now that the trail turned to the southwest, the terrain also changed. With the mountains looming to the west, and the Oregon Buttes to the south, the land was marked with multiple dry creek beds that handled the spring runoff and the sudden cloudbursts of summer that caused flash floods as the water sought escape to the Sweetwater drainage. A long rimrocked topped ridge was cut by the Sweetwater at the confluence with Chimney Creek and Spring Creek, but the wagon trail crossed the river and took to the northwest, dropping from the wide plateau to the more rugged terrain of the low foothills that marked the southern tip of the Wind River Mountains.

Once away from the ridge, Morgan's planned stop was to be near a couple of small shallow lakes, but he was surprised to see six freight wagons circled nearby, and a herd of mules staked out near the lakes. He rode ahead to meet the freighters and was greeted by a tall, well set-up man with a Lindsey Woolsey shirt under wide galluses and tucked into canvas britches atop heavy hobnail boots. He lifted one hand to wave to Morgan and motioned him to join him at the fire for some coffee.

"Howdy friend, I'm Thomas Wannamaker, and I'm boss o' this outfit. We're headin' to Salt Lake by way o' Fort Bridger! How 'bout you folks?"

Morgan stepped down, extended his hand to shake, "Howdy. I'm Jeremiah Morgan, most just call me Morgan. We're headed to Oregon, lookin' to find some good farm land and build us a new home."

"Wal, have yer'self some coffee, friend. Were you plannin' on campin' here, it is gettin' on towards sundown."

"That was the plan until I saw your camp. We don't wanna crowd you none, so if you'd prefer, we can keep goin'."

"No, no, no reason for that. There's plenty o' room. Don't look like you got'churself more'n what, fifteen wagons?"

"That's right, and we'd be pleased to camp here, I'll have 'em circle up yonder," he pointed to a flat grassy area about fifty yards from the freighters camp, "an' we'll stake our mules out on beyond."

"That'd be fine, fine. An' after you get settled, come on back an' we'll chew the fat a spell," suggested Wannamaker.

Morgan stood, stretched out his hand to shake again, "Thanks friend, we're needin' a day or two of rest, been pushin' hard to get shed o' them Indians."

Wannamaker stood looking somewhat alarmed, "Injuns?"

"Yeah, we were hit by a Crow raidin' party a couple days ago, but we run 'em off. Only lost one man, so we did alright."

Wannamaker nodded his head, thoughtful, and added, "Uh, you be sure to come back an' sit a spell after you get set. We need to talk 'bout them Injuns."

"Sure, sure. Won't be long," answered Morgan and mounted back up to direct the wagons to their campsite. Since the attack, the people of the wagons were more cooperative and responsive to his leadership, and with just a few hand signals, the wagons circled up as directed and the men began unhitching the teams. Morgan walked from wagon to wagon, assigning the tasks of guard duty, herd duty, and cautioning everyone about wandering away. As he came to Charley's wagon, the one shared by him, Smitty the scout, and Charley, the old mountain man asked, "So, how long we gonna be hyar?"

"Well, from here on up we've got a pretty steady climb an' I thought it'd be good to take at least a day to rest the mules, 'fore we give it a try. Don'tchu think?"

Charley nodded his head and looked toward the freighters, "Them fellers been hyar long?"

"I'm not sure, I think they just pulled in today, mebbe last night. Why?"

"I was thinkin' it might be a good idea to tag along wit' 'em, case we run into more Injuns!"

Morgan looked back toward the freight wagons and

turned back to the old man, "Ya' know, Charley," and paused, looking to the wiry mountain man, "what is your last name anyway, you never said?"

He cackled before answering, "Ain't got one!"

Morgan leaned back and scowled, "Whaddaya mean, ain't got one. Ever'body's got a last name!"

"Nope, ya' see, I was raised in an orphanage, never knew who muh ma and pa was, and never took any other name. Allus been called Charley. If there was any'thin' resemblin' a last name it would be 'Just Charley'."

Morgan's forehead wrinkled as he peered from under bushy brows and Charley continued, "Wal, I give folks muh name as Charley, just Charley, so they thinks muh last name's 'Just Charley'! Hehehee."

Morgan shook his head, grinning, and answered, "Yeah, I think it might be a good idea to join up with the freighters. They are goin' over South Pass and on to Salt Lake, so we'll be coverin' some o' the same country and it would be safer with more men and rifles. I'm goin' over there in a bit, and I'll talk to 'em about it."

"Good, good. There's sumpin' else. I was thinkin' 'bout takin' this time to go check on Tate's family, like he asked. An' I could see 'bout them youngsters too, if ya want."

"Sure, that'd be good. I talked to the Johnston's about the young'uns, and they were interested but non-committal. I think they'd like to meet 'em first."

"Sounds fair. The kids prob'ly wanna meet them too." He looked up to the west to judge how much daylight was left and looked back to Morgan, "Looks to me like I got a couple hours left, so I might just oughta head on out, ya' reckon?"

"Sure, if we leave 'fore you get back, I'll have Smitty drive the wagon. You can find us, I'm sure."

Charley waved over his shoulder as he turned to fetch his gear before he unhitched the mule team. His horse had been with the herd of spare mules and other horses used by the pilgrims on their hunting forays. He started whistling as he stepped lively around his duties, anxious to be off on his own and heading to the timber.

———

BAD HEART BEAR rode beside Pretty Eagle as they crossed the Popo Agie River, once across Bear turned to Pretty Eagle, "We will camp this night where the Little Popo Agie breaks the long ridge of red. At first light, you will take two hands of warriors and go up to the lake, then follow the trail to South Pass. You will come to the trail before the wagons and attack them from the trees as they come to you. I will take the others and we will move along the red ridge and come to the wagons from behind." He used his hands to motion the directions and emphasize the direction. "They will not know of this and we can attack before they have their shoots far rifles ready!" he declared as if him saying it would make it true. "You will attack from the south of the river, we will come from the north at the crossing of the river."

"It is good. It will take one day to ride, we will attack at first light on the next day?" asked Pretty Eagle.

Bear nodded curtly, grinning, and pleased with his plan. He knew this time they would destroy all the wagons and capture many prisoners and take many supplies. The council would be pleased, his men would gain honors, and he would lead many more war parties. He smiled and nodded to himself, proud of his work and his coming victory.

TATE AND WHISKERS AGREED ON A BIG DAPPLE-GRAY gelding and Tate began transferring his gear from Shady. Whiskers asked, "Could ya' use some comp'ny on this little free for all ya' got planned?"

Tate looked at the whiskery face and thought for a moment, "I reckon we could use some help, if you think you're up to it?"

The big man grinned and nodded, "Good, good, I was gettin' a little bored 'round here anyhoo. It'll be good to unlimber ol' Betsy. Don't wanna see her gettin' rusty." Betsy was a .54 caliber Hawken that was well used, and Whiskers took pride in his marksmanship with the rifle. He added, "Wouldn't s'prise me none if ol' Red Pipe an' some his warriors don't wanna come along too. There's been talk 'bout gettin' up a war party an' gettin' some revenge on them Crows. This might jus' be what he's been wantin'."

Tate stopped and looked at the man, "You think he'd do that?"

"Ummhumm, he's got him quite a name as a warrior. Cain't hardly see his coup stick fer all them scalps on it. So, 'fore ya' finish gearin' up that horse, mebbe we should go talk to Red Pipe, whatsay?"

Tate lifted his eyes to the sky to determine how much daylight was left, looked back to Whiskers and said, "Mebbe you're right. Sun's 'bout ta' go down, it's 'bout half a day or so to the cabin, so, let's see what Red Pipe's thinkin'."

As Whiskers suspected, Red Pipe had spoken with his council and all were in agreement that a move against the Crow at this time was needed. Since the Crow were moving into the territory of the Arapaho, making raids on the white wagons at South Pass, the council saw this as a challenge to their people. The Crow had historically kept to the Absaroka and the Bighorn mountains and making their raids into the land of the Arapaho was an affront to the power of the Bäsawunena and the challenge must be met, and the people avenged.

"We will go against the Apsáalooke, these children of the large-beaked bird, the ones who made their mark on a treaty with the whites to stay in the Big Horn mountains, and now come into our lands and attack us and show their scorn for the Bäsawunena people. We will chase them back to their land, if we do not kill them all!" Red Pipe was standing and speaking forcefully so those that stood behind him would know of his determination. "I will lead our people!" he shouted as he raised his fist in the air. He turned and gestured toward Tate, "Longbow and Big Bear will go with us to take them before they strike against the white mans' wagons!"

Tate looked to Whiskers and mouthed the words, 'Big

Bear?' and received a grin from the whiskery apparition of a grizzly. Tate chuckled and looked to Red Pipe, "When you wanna leave?"

"We will be on the trail before first light!"

Tate nodded his understanding and agreement, thinking that would put them to his cabin by midday and allow time to make it to South Pass before nightfall. His mission was twofold, make sure his family was safe, and locate the Crow war party and warn the wagon train.

———

"STRAWBERRY CREEK CUTS away from the Sweetwater right after them two little lakes most folks camp by, goes mostly west 'fore it turns north after 'bout five miles or so. Foller that til it peters out an' head straight north till ya' come to the tree line. The trail you want cuts due north thru them trees." Those were the directions Tate had given Charley when he asked the old-timer to check on his family. Charley was grinning widely as he rocked to the gait of his horse, hearing only the creak of saddle leather, the clomp of his horse's hooves, and the chuckling of the stream on his left.

The sun had dropped behind the mountains to the west but still colored the scattered clouds as it dipped its rays into the gold and orange colors of its palette. Charley watched as the paint of sundown filled the western sky and made the hillsides glow. A rambunctious fox was turning somersaults as it courted a watching vixen. His antics had drawn an audience of a jackrabbit sitting on his big hind feet with his tall ears erect, a coyote that trotted by, and a pair of whiskey jacks. It was wilderness entertainment at its finest and no admission charge. Once the tod fox cozied up to the vixen, the acrobatics were replaced by chin rubs and sniffing, and the audience that soon faded into the background. Charley pushed on, wanting to get to the trees before he made camp. He wasn't hungry and would probably just have some coffee and chew on some jerky.

He wove his way through the scattered juniper and cedar and finally crested the slope by the fading twilight. A few moments later and he was into the darker timber. He found a suitable campsite near a downed and grayed trunk of a big ponderosa, and was soon leaning back with a steaming cup of java in his hands. He looked to the darkening sky, picked out a few early stars and with a deep breath of satisfaction, he tossed the dregs of his coffee on the smoldering coals and slid down into his blankets for a long-awaited sleep. Morning would come soon enough, and he would be back on the trail to the cabin and family of Tate Saint. He grinned at the thought of being back in the deep timber and enjoying the smell of high country air with the spruce and fir.

———

IT WAS by the light of the stirred-up fire that the Crow war party readied themselves. Little was said as the party split with the larger group following Bad Heart Bear into the red-walled canyon. Pretty Eagle, Spotted Horse, and Buffalo Horn were followed by ten warriors as they started up to the trail above the Little Popo Agie. Their trail was well carpeted with pine needles and matted aspen leaves, and the thirteen riders moved almost noiselessly. When the trail rose to follow the canyon, they moved single-file on the narrow winding game trail, but they made good time. Pretty Eagle dispatched Spotted Horse and Buffalo Horn to scout ahead, and the two gigged their horses to a trot as they disappeared around the shoulder of the mountain.

The two scouts moved quickly and quietly along the shoulder below the bald mesa top, but the movement startled a bunch of bighorn sheep that scampered up the mountainside, sending rocks cascading to the trail below. The trail dropped through an aspen cluttered notch and to the valley of the Little Popo Agie where the confluence with two other streams added to the flow. They rode over to the smaller stream that came from the lake and followed the oft-crossed game trail through the thicker timber. They slowed as they neared the lake and the timber dwindled to scrub oak brush amidst basaltic rock that fell from a talus that narrowed the trail at lakeside. The scouts slid from their mounts and climbed the slope to scan the area. On the far side of the lake, where the tall timber skirted the larger mountain behind, a thin trail of smoke was seen. Spotted Horse pointed it out and Buffalo Horn pointed to the lake shore where two people, apparently young, were walking. "Whites," said Horn.

Spotted Horse shaded his eyes, leaning forward and searched the area from his vantage point, "A cabin," he said as he pointed to the thin smoke. He turned to Buffalo Horn, "Go, tell Pretty Eagle, I will scout the cabin and be here when you return."

Horn nodded, slid down the slope and soon disappeared in the thick buck-brush. With another searching look to determine his course, Spotted Horse went to his mount and began his reconnoiter.

It was but an hour later when the band of Crow led by Pretty Eagle came to the Talus and the waiting Spotted Horse. "One woman, four younger. Two older are one girl and one boy, close to warrior age. Young are girl and boy. No man."

Pretty Eagle had mounted the talus to see the far side of the lake and he turned quickly to ask, "No man?"

Horse nodded his head, "No man."

———

TATE RODE alongside Red Pipe as they followed the trail south toward the lake and cabin. They had been on the trail well over an hour when the sun started to peek above the eastern mountains and cast its gaze where they rode. The trail climbed from the Arapaho camp and rounding a knob of the mountain, it traversed a steep timber covered slope about halfway up the mountainside. After rounding another shoulder, they broke into a high park with a boggy peat moss bottomed lake bed. They made a slight climb over a saddle into another park, but this one held a nice sized lake surrounded on three sides with tall timber that came clear to the waterline. The crystal-clear water showed blue in the mountain air and was inviting to the tired animals, prompting the entourage to move to the rocky shore and let the them drink. The men stepped down to stretch their legs and most dug into parfleches or bags and brought out pemmican or jerky for a quick rest.

The small lake was behind them as they moved into the thicker timber and strung out on the narrow trail.

Lobo was in the lead and suddenly stopped in place, a stance recognized by Tate. Red Pipe moved beside Tate and whispered, "Does he see a rabbit or something?"

"No, there's trouble," answered Tate, watching Lobo. The wolf raised his head, testing the air, ears pricked forward and abruptly turned his head back to Tate, snarled with a curled lip, and took off at a run. Tate instantly dug heels into the dapple-gray and the horse leaped forward bringing the lead line to Shady tight and both horses took off at a full run, Tate leaning low on the neck of the gray but reaching behind him to slip the Sharps from the scabbard.

CHAPTER SEVENTEEN
FIGHT

"To the house, now! Run!" hollered Sean to Ira and Vicky. He motioned with his arm and hollered again, "Now! Hurry!" Seeing the scared look on the boy's face and the urgency in his voice, they started at a run up the slope to the cabin. Sean ran behind them, turned and took another quick look, and followed them onto the porch and into the house. Sean slammed the door and went to the shutters as he hollered to his Mom, "Indians! And they ain't friendly!" Maggie went to the other window, closed and latched the shutters and went to check the window in the bedroom.

"What's goin' on?" asked Vicky, still standing by the door.

"I saw a couple Indians 'cross the lake, one rode off and the other started to come around thisaway." As he spoke he started up the ladder to the loft, going for his Hawken and possibles.

When he came back down, Maggie asked, "How many did you see and where were they?"

"Two Ma, and they had paint. They were by that talus slope on the south shore, but one of 'em left and the other started around the lake this way."

"How'd you see them?"

Sean chuckled and answered, "Well, I had shimmied up that big spruce there by the shore. I was gonna scare them two," motioning to Ira and Vicky, "when they came under it, but I looked around an' saw the Indians. I don't think they saw me but I'm purty sure they saw them two," he said. The two newcomers were out for a walk and were talking about what they might do with their lives but having no idea as to what might be possible. Although they had been friendly with one another while on the wagon train, they never really spent much time together, but now they only had one another and were becoming quite close.

Ira asked, "Is there another rifle?"

Maggie had brought out her Sharps and laid it on the table, checking the load and her pouch of paper cartridges and percussion caps. She looked up and said, "Yes, just inside the door," nodding toward the bedroom door.

Ira fetched the other Hawken and possibles pouch and powder horn and sat down to check its load and cap. He looked to the pouch for balls and caps, and satisfied, slipped the powder horn over his head and the possibles bag to the opposite side from the horn. Once Maggie was set, she positioned Sean at the other front window, Ira at the side window and told Vicky, "I'll need you to keep an eye on Sadie, once shooting starts, you two go to the bedroom and keep watch, because they might try coming around back and I need you to watch, but just through the firing slots, to see if they try that. Understand?"

"Yes ma'am, I can do that," answered Vicky, and turned to go to Sadie who was sitting against the wall, holding her doll and watching the others bustling around. She sat beside the younger girl, smiled, and slipped an arm around her shoulders.

Maggie was confident in her skill with the Sharps, she and Tate had used them often and her marksmanship rivaled that of her husband's. They had both become very adept at judging distances and adjusting their aim to compensate and she now opened the shooting slot in the heavy window shutters and searched for her first target. Based on where Sean first saw them and knowing the trails around the lake, she guessed they would come around both sides and try to attack the cabin. The trail on the south bank was easier and would probably draw the most warriors and perhaps the leaders. Maggie picked a couple of places that would make good targets if the Indians showed themselves, and she was certain they would, especially if they had scouted the cabin. If they believed there was only one woman and four youngsters, they might get a little careless and make themselves a target for her Sharps.

Her first mark was a lone big trunked spruce, about four hundred yards and easily seen by the lighter covered bark, and near the trail with low branches that would make any rider swing wide and right into Maggie's line of sight. Her second mark was a boulder at about three hundred yards that would probably attract for the cover it offered, but they would have to come out from behind it to attack. As she continued to watch, she spoke to both the boys, "Pick yourselves a mark at about two hundred yards and another about one hundred. Make sure the mark is near the trail or clearing that they might come through, and ready yourselves to take your first shot when your target comes alongside. Understand?"

"Yeah, Ma. Already got a couple picked out," answered Sean, confidently.

"Yes'm, will do," answered Ira, a little less certain.

"And have your next ball an' patch ready close at hand," encouraged Maggie, with a calm voice. "Take your time and pick your target, and get ready, cuz, here they come!"

It was just a moment later when the big Sharps roared and bucked in Maggie's hands and the fight was on. She watched for just a couple seconds as she blindly dropped the lever and opened the breech on the Sharps and saw the painted warrior flip backwards off his horse, making the others take to the timber.

———

EVEN AT A FULL RUN, the dapple had little trouble maneuvering through the timber on the narrow trail. Tate leaned low along the horse's neck, but the sound of the rifle shot brought him up and he pulled the horse to a stop. He paused to listen and look through the trees. He knew he was nearing the cabin, but he had to be careful as he approached; he had to know what was happening. He wasn't close enough to see and gigged his horse forward at a trot, Tate standing in his stirrups and moving side to side trying to see through the thicker pines.

He caught a glimpse of a horseman, moved forward to see better and recognized the man as a Crow warrior moving along the trail, watching the action below him and nearer the cabin. Tate reined the gray into the thicker trees, dropped to the ground and loosely tied both the gray and Shady. He had motioned Lobo back to his side and Tate quickly pulled the longbow from the sheath and strung it, hooked his quiver to his belt, and with the rifle slung over his back, he stepped into the trees and closer to the cabin.

Sporadic gunfire came from the cabin and a few of the warriors with rifles. Tate was relieved to see the cabin closed up tight and rifle barrels protruding from the gun ports. The warrior he spotted before had also tethered his horse and was starting to approach the cabin, but Tate quickly nocked an arrow and let it fly true to its mark piercing the warrior through the back and knocking him to his face in the pine needles, never to move again. He was determined to take a considerable tally before they knew he was there, wanting to turn the odds in his favor and prevent the Indians breach of the cabin. But as Tate searched the area for another target, he saw two warriors moving toward the back of the cabin and out of sight of the bedroom window. He dropped his bow, bringing his Sharps abruptly around and in one smooth movement. He sighted on the closest one to the cabin and squeezed off his shot that knocked the warrior off his feet and flattened him against the corner corral post to drop in a heap. The shot had startled the second attacker, who turned and caught Tate's second shot in his chest to blossom red on his vest as he was knocked to the ground. Tate smiled and thought to himself that he was glad he practiced with the quick reloading of the paper cartridges for the Sharps, it was certainly paying off.

·   ·   ·

MAGGIE HEARD the reports of the Sharps and when Vicky called out, "Somebody just shot two Indians near the back!", she knew it was Tate. She smiled and said, "I think your pa's out there Sean!"

"He is? Wow, just in time too!" and squeezed off his first shot at a charging warrior. When the band mounted their attack, they chose to make the approach silently, but once the rifles barked their protest, war cries sounded and a few of the younger warriors trying to show their bravery, jumped from cover and charged the cabin screaming their war cries.

Suddenly another Sharps barked, but this one from the trees by the trail leading to the south and away from the cabin. But this Sharps was just as accurate as the others, and another Crow buc caught in running stride, twisted in the air and fell to his face, his scream choking on blood. The Sharps from the cabin echoed the one from the trail, and another boomed from the trees on the hillside.

Unexpectedly, war cries and the thunder of hooves came from behind Tate and he turned quickly, thinking the attack was now coming from the hillside. But he was surprised to see Red Pipe leading his warriors as they streamed through the trees to attack the Crow who were attacking on foot. Now the remaining Crow turned and ran through the brush and trees, trying to escape the charging Arapaho. Tate ran to the cabin, hollering to those inside, "Don't shoot! Don't shoot!" as he ran up on the porch. He pushed open the door, caught Maggie as she jumped into his arms, and said to Sean and Ira, "Don't shoot! Those are Arapaho and they're friendly, at least to us. They'll take care of the rest of the Crow."

Maggie said, "Wait, you were up on the hillside, who's shooting from the trail? It was a Sharps too!"

Tate looked at her and to the door, he stepped on the porch, Sharps in hand and bow across his back, turned back to the cabin, "Shut the door, that's a friend and I gotta make sure he don't shoot the Arapaho!"

He quickly scanned the trees and trail before the cabin, looked to the lakeside beyond and saw several Arapaho scuffling with some of the Crow, but none seemed to be going into the trees by the trail. He started at a trot along the trail, making the sound of a nighthawk, knowing if it was Charley, as he suspected, the old mountain man would be wary and watchful but not quick to shoot. Within a short distance, he saw the wiry old man step from behind a tree and grin at Tate as he dropped his Sharps to his side.

"Wal, that was fun!" cackled the white whiskers. "Hold on thar while I get muh horse," he spoke as he turned away and started back into the trees. He soon re-appeared leading his horse and came to Tate to shake his hand. "That had to be the wildest welcome I ever had!" His eyes twinkled with amusement and he waddled bow-legged beside Tate along the trail. Both men held their rifles at the ready and watched the trees and brush for any lurking Crow as Tate told Charley about the friendly Arapaho and the old man said, "I kinda figgered they was on our side when they chased them others into the brush and started scalpin' 'em."

Tate saw the big form of Whiskers coming from the trail beside the lake and stood waiting for the man. His whiskers parted as he grinned at Tate and said, "I think ol' Red Pipe and them others are havin' themselves a good time with a couple them Crow. They got 'em back there in the trees and are sorta explainin' why they don't like Crows." He chuckled as he dismounted and greeted Charley with a handshake that made the old man's hand disappear in his massive paw.

"Well, I hope Red Pipe don't take too long, this ain't the main bunch. I'm still thinkin' they might be after the wagon train," said Tate as they neared the porch of the cabin. He started to call out to Maggie, but Charley grabbed his arm and asked, "You mean there's a bigger bunch an' they're after the wagons?"

Tate nodded and answered, "That's right, we're on our way to meet up with 'em and see if we can't stop the Crow, once and for all."

Charley turned and drew his horse near and said, "You fellas come along when you can, I'm goin' on to let 'em know you're comin'. And, there's more of 'em, we joined up with some freighters, so them Crow don't know what they're up against!" He swung aboard and reined around to start back up the trail at a canter, waving over his shoulder to Tate and company.

SEAN AND IRA VOLUNTEERED TO FETCH TATE'S TWO HORSES
and soon returned to the cabin. Tate introduced Whiskers
and Red Pipe to Maggie, explained their mission and was
sent on his way with a fresh supply of jerky, smoked meat,
biscuits and a kiss and a hug from Maggie. Red Pipe had
dispatched Broken Lance and another to scout out the
trail before them and to try to locate the main party of the
Crow. And by midday, Tate, Whiskers and the Arapaho
were back on the trail.

As they traveled, Tate was silent as he turned over in
his mind what he knew of the Crow. He had been
surprised to encounter the party that attacked his cabin,
but as he considered it, he believed this group was trying
to circle around and come at the wagon train from the
front. Last time, when the train was attacked on South
Pass, they had taken the travelers by surprise and over-
whelmed them before they could mount a reasonable
defense. That tactic had worked well for them and their
leader, who Tate believed was not with this group but

with the larger band, would use the same strategy for his revenge on this group of wagons. *What was it Charley had said? Oh yeah, they had joined up with a group of freighters!* Tate knew that freight wagons carried more goods, but also more armed men. He didn't know how many freighters there were, but even a small group would probably double the number of rifles. But the Crow chief would not know this until his men scouted the train and reported back, but by that time, there would be no way for him to get word to the second group he was expecting to come from the front of the wagons, but that group was no more.

Tate considered the terrain of the summit of South Pass. There was nothing near the trail that would provide much cover except the rolling hills. With the only vegetation being bunch grass, sage and cacti, the only way a band of attackers could be hidden was for them to be on foot and secreted behind the sage and grease wood. And what would be the best place for an attack? Especially, considering there would have to be a place where both bands could have an advantage? In his mind's eye, he scanned the area of South Pass, focusing on that part near the crest. The entire area was rolling hills, a few small feeder streams, little vegetation and only a few scattered juniper, piñon and cedar trees. But along the banks of the Sweetwater were thicker growths of willow, alder, and stunted cottonwood. Of course, the crossing at the bend of the river when the headwaters came from the north and turned to the east.

Tate turned to Red Pipe and shared his thoughts, "You're familiar with this country, don't you think the crossing would be the best place for an ambush?"

Red Pipe looked at Tate, considered what he had said, and answered, "That would be the place I would choose. With two bands to attack, one could come from the south and be hidden in the brush across the river, and the other could come from behind, probably hidden in one of the low places beyond the hills. Yes, I would choose that place."

The southern end of the Wind River range was marked by a string of granite topped peaks that marched away to the north like gray uniformed soldiers in a row. The crest of that ridge dropped away to the south, made a dog leg bend to the east and again pointed southward with three lesser peaks that rose to just below timberline before the shoulder of the ridge pointed south and faded away under the black timber. Beyond the timber covered hills, the terrain was marked by many ravines, some water in small streams, and rocky hills that changed the course of the runoff streams by their basaltic barriers. The last two streams that came from the foothills of the Winds were Pine Creek and Fish Creek, with Fish Creek being the last crossing for the wagon trail before it reached the banks of the Sweetwater and the last crossing before the crest of the pass.

It was nearing dusk when the entourage of Arapaho came to the edge of the black timber and overlooked the rolling foothills that stretched toward the distant Oregon Buttes in the south. Tate suggested, "How 'bout we wait til near dark, then move on down to Fish Creek to make camp for the night. That will put us closer to the trail and make it easier to intercept the Crow."

"It is good!" agreed Red Pipe and slid from his mount. The rest of the party of Arapaho followed the example of their chief and let their horses graze on the nearby buffalo grass and gramma. Most of the men found their comfort sitting down and leaning against a tree or a boulder, some even reclined on the grass to await the coming darkness. Tate knew they wouldn't have a fire in camp for the night, so he chose to dig out some pemmican and eat his fill.

When the colors of sunset had faded from the western sky, the group of Arapaho were ready to move. Tate suggested, "Red Pipe, we need to know where the Crow are, and we also need to know where the wagons are, so, I'm thinkin' I can take Broken Lance with me and scout the Crow, and we can send Whiskers to find the wagons. That way the people with the wagons will know what we're up to and won't be shootin' at you and your men, and we'll have a better idea 'bout the Crow and if we were right in what we guessed about their plans."

"It is good. We will camp on Fish Creek, above the wagon trail. You can send Lance back with your word," answered Red Pipe.

Tate motioned to Broken Lance and Whiskers and as the men came near, Tate nodded to Red Pipe and the three rode into the night. The moon was waning from full, now showing a bit more than a three quarter and provided ample light for the travel. Tate looked to the sky, scattered clouds were as black shadows to hide the stars, but he saw the constellation of Orion and grinned at the thought of the mighty hunter. The three scouts moved silently through the night, bound for the Oregon Trail and beyond to find the tracks of the Crow war party.

With just over an hour behind them, they came to the wagon trail and turned to ride back toward the wagons and freighters. But after a couple of miles, Tate spoke to

Whiskers, "We'll part here. You go on and let the wagon-master, name o' Morgan, know what's happening. Charley probably already told 'em there was an attack comin' but they don't know 'bout us an' the Arapaho. We're thinkin' the attack'll come at the crossing of the Sweetwater, so be sure to let them boys know not to shoot at the Arapaho. Most o' them Crow have that pompadour top knot,

but that ain't so easy to see in the middle of a fight. But do what'chu can. When we find the Crow, I'll send Lance here back to tell Red Pipe, an' if there's anything special, he might stop off to tell you."

"Alright, I'll talk to these fellers, an' you keep your top-knot on, ya hear?" answered Whiskers, grinning at Tate.

"You too, my friend."

They nodded to one another and gigged their horses on their appointed course, both disappearing into the darkness. Tate and Lance angled off from the wagon trail, looking to intersect the tracks of the Crow war party. But in the dim moonlight, they had to ride careful and quiet. Sound carried in the darkness and for anyone listening, that change in the usual night sounds caused by someone passing, was a dead giveaway of their presence. As they rode across the grassy rolling hills, the only sounds to be heard was the clatter of the cicadas, an occasional yip yip of a coyote and more rarely, the howl of a wolf. Once when a distant howl was heard, Lobo stopped and listened, then answered with a long yowl that rose and dropped off as he lowered his head and the lonesome call was soon answered by the first wolf. It was not the cry of a challenge, but rather of the announcement of a lovesick female and Lobo looked back at Tate as if asking permission to search her out, but Tate did not respond, and Lobo continued his long loping trot that let him move silently through the night.

Suddenly Lobo stopped, slowly turned his head to look back at Tate, and the two men reined their horses to a stop and slipped to the ground. They used a nearby sage to tether their mounts and together started up the low rise to see what Lobo had spotted. They bellied down as they neared the crest and slowly crawled to the top, lifted their heads just enough to look beyond, and there in the bottom of the swale, a horse herd and the many still forms of sleeping bodies. They had no fire and there was the smallest trickle of water that snaked through the bottom, but it was enough for their horses and their own use. Small long hills rose beyond and Tate noted this was an excellent place for the entire war party to hide. Not far from the wagon trail, but totally obscured from sight. Even if one of the men from the wagons were to use a telescope, they could not see this camp that lay below the rise of the surrounding hills.

Their trail had paralleled that of the wagons but was below the river. And knowing the crossing of the Sweetwater was less than three miles ahead, this war party could easily mount their attack as soon as the wagons neared, and the wagon trail could be seen from the top of the knoll to the north of their camp. Tate and Lance slid back down the low rise and Tate sent Lance back to tell the wagons and Red Pipe. He whispered, "I'm gonna follow 'em and maybe give 'em a little surprise." Lance didn't ask any questions, just quietly mounted up and left.

CHAPTER NINETEEN
READINESS

As he watched Lance ride into the darkness on his mission of warning, Tate slipped the longbow from the sheath and drew one arrow from the quiver. He strung the bow and started back up the low rising knoll that overlooked the Crow camp. He bellied down as he crested it and looked below to the camp, judging the distance and placement of the sleepers. He searched the surrounding area for any warriors on guard and seeing none, he slowly stood up just behind the crest of the knoll and nocked an arrow. As he stood, he could still see the sleepers and the horse herd, but he had not sky-lined himself for any unseen guards. He calculated his shot, leaned into the bow and brought it to full draw, lifted the tip just a mite and let the arrow fly. The shaft quickly whispered away and out of sight, but in Tate's mind's eye, he knew it would arch just a little and slowly drop to impale itself amidst the sleepers. He leaned forward, dropping to his knees and watched for any movement. There was none.

Tate grinned to himself as he pictured the reaction of

the warriors when they awoke and saw another black arrow in their midst. He walked back down the slope and mounted up, choosing a wide circle below and around the war party where he would search for his lookout point in anticipation of the attack shortly after dawn.

The moonlight was bright enough of a silvery blanket for the rolling hills that appeared as fuzzy knobs in the dim glow of just after midnight. The shadowy ravine marked the draw that harbored the narrow creek that was called Fish Creek even though it held barely enough water for a few frogs. He spotted what he wanted, and it appeared to be lighted by the stars at the very crest. The hillock was topped with a patch of alkali that shone white in the moonlight. He would make this his promontory and shooting stand for the coming fight. The dry creek bed just east of the knob would provide protection for Shady, he had left the gray with the Arapaho, and Lobo would be with him at his promontory. But for now, he chose to make his bed with Shady in the dry draw and get a bit of rest before everything started.

―――――

"So, this place where Tate thinks the Crow will attack, is it the same spot they attacked the other wagons?" Morgan asked Whiskers.

"No, don't think so. That fight was closer to where we are now, just past that next draw I b'lieve. But Tate was thinkin' they'd want a place where they could surprise ya' and there's more cover down in the bottom o' that crossin'."

Thomas Wannamaker, the boss of the freighters, spoke

up, "I know that crossin' and it would be a good place fer an ambush. We'd be busy crossin' the bogs an' stream, an' they could hit us 'fore we'd ever get to our guns!"

"So, how're we gonna tell the differ'nce 'tween these Arapaho and them Crow?" asked Morgan.

Whiskers grinned and squirmed a little, "Wal, we figger them Crow'll be comin' from the front an' expectin' their pards to be comin' up behind ya', what they don't know is their pards is all done in, and them whut'll be comin' from behind'ja will be the Arapahos. So, just don't shoot any o' them whut comes from behind'ja. And they'll be takin' off after them Crows, so, pick your shots then."

Morgan looked to Wannamaker and asked, "Do you wanna lead out with your freighters?"

Wannamaker grinned, "Yup, shore do. Ya see, each o' them wagons got not just the muleskinner, but they got a extry man with a rifle always ready. And most of 'em have two. That's mainly to handle the cargo, but they have rifles too. So, we can have them keep their heads down an' give them Crow a little surprise."

Morgan looked to Whiskers and asked, "But what if they hit us from the rear, what then?"

"I'd say ya' need to have a few extry shooters in the back wagons."

Morgan thought about it a moment and started to speak when Charley piped up, "Why cain't we just circle the wagons 'fore we cross the crick, an' make the Injuns come after us?"

Morgan looked to Charley, then back to Wannamaker and Whiskers and said, "Why can't we?" The question was directed at the group and the men looked from one to another. Morgan added, "Wannamaker, you know the area better'n the rest of us, you think it'd be better to circle up first?"

The freighter boss thought about it for a moment, then said, "Couple miles 'fore we get to the crossin' we cross over a little crick, I think it's called Fish Crick, but from there to the crossin' there ain't a place big 'nuff to circle the wagons. An' fer the last half mile, it's a long slope, kinda a side slope, down to the crossin' and couldn't really circle up. But if they was to attack 'fore we get to the crossin' we could double up, ya' know, pull up alongside one another."

The men continued their discussion and idea sharing into the night, but nothing was settled when slumber beckoned, and everyone turned in before the coming battle.

LOBO NUDGED Tate awake well before the first light shone from the eastern flats. He checked on Shady, tethered him close to the trickle of water and some grass, then he started up the knoll with Lobo at his side. With one hand holding the Sharps, the longbow across his back, the quiver of arrows at his side, and the possibles bag with ammo over his shoulder, Tate was armed for the battle. The moon hung just above the western mountains and the stars were beginning their retreat when he crested the knob. He had no cover other than his elevation above the narrow draw that held Fish Creek and his view of the Sweetwater crossing. He judged the middle of the crossing to be about three hundred yards and he suspected the Crow would use the creek-side brush and stunted trees for their cover.

Now, if I was attacking, I'd wanna hit 'em just as they come to the water, or back a ways when they're fightin' that slope comin' down to the crick. Mebbe I'd put a few men along the bottom o' Fish Crick here, an' over yonder on the other side o' the wagon road. He looked at Lobo and whispered, "Ya don't think he'd try to put somebody up here on this mound, do ya? Nah, this is too far away for any o' their rifles." Lobo looked back at him, wagged his tail and smiled with his tongue lolling to the side at his friend. "But ya know boy, we might be a little conspicuous up here." He looked around for anything to use as cover or to mask their presence, but there were no rocks, bushes, or anything obvious. He looked at the white alkali and knew what would work.

He lay down in the alkali and rolled over and back again, picking up some of the chalky dust and rubbed it on the back of his buckskins. Another couple of handfuls were used to rub into Lobo's coat, which the wolf wasn't too happy about but since Tate set the example, he tolerated this unusual antic of his friend. Tate stretched out on his belly, took aim at the suspected positions of the enemy, lay his possibles bag before him and placed several paper cartridges on the bag within easy reach, alongside a handful of percussion caps, then lay his rifle down and brought his telescope to his eye to search the area below.

The sky was just threatening to show the first dim light of gray when Tate saw movement. He turned his scope to the confluence of the Sweetwater and Fish Creek to see several warriors on foot and scattering to cover. "Here they come boy, musta picketed their horses back down the draw a ways, that's good," he whispered to Lobo as he watched the Crow war party pick their places. He watched about half of them move across the wagon trail and to the slight rise on the far side, where there was just enough of a rise with a drop off behind to give cover for the attackers.

The others were lining themselves out along the bottom of Fish Creek and moving closer to his bald knob. He chuckled as he whispered, "That's it, come on now, just a little closer, make it easy on Tate an' Lobo," and watched several warriors line out along the bank nearest the wagon trail. He wanted to find the leader of the group, but apparently, he had learned his lesson at the last attack and was either staying well back or had joined his warriors and was unrecognizable. The slight bank and scattering of willows and alders would be ample cover for their attack. Tate whispered to Lobo, "Well, boy, now it's just wait. Looks like they're gonna hit the wagons 'fore they get to the crossin' and come at 'em from both sides. Sure hope Whiskers made it to warn 'em. Otherwise, we're gonna be almighty busy."

Tate was about to lower his scope when he saw a rider coming at a canter, apparently searching for someone. He moved toward the warriors on the far side then suddenly reined up and dropped from his horse, running to the side of one of the attackers. Tate watched through his scope and saw the rider speaking to a sizable man with a pompadour and scalplock with long braids interwoven with beaver fur. Tate grinned as he recognized this was the leader, now he just needed a good shot at the man responsible for so many deaths, but that would have to wait until the attack.

———

BAD HEART BEAR stood when he saw the mounted warrior coming toward him. This would be the scout he sent out before first light. Crazy Fox slipped to the ground and approached Bear, "The wagons are moving, and there are more! There are big wagons, that carry much goods, that are with the others!" Fox was excited to bring the news that the train would have more goods to take, more than they had expected.

Bear was stoic when he heard the report, "And the others?" he asked, concerned about the rest of the war party under Pretty Eagle.

"I saw their camp, they are in the creek bed beyond the road, as we expected. I could not signal them, but they are ready."

Bear grinned at the report. He believed with the two bands attacking, one at the front and the other at the rear, their victory was assured. Bear looked at Fox and said, "Take your horse to the others, and return here to fight."

What the Crow leader did not know was the camp spotted by Crazy Fox was the camp of the Arapaho and not Pretty Eagle, who had been killed with his men in his attack on the cabin by the lake, and Pretty Eagle and his band would not be there for his two-pronged attack. Fox was excited about the coming battle and to be asked to fight beside their leader was an honor. He hurried to take his horse to be picketed with the others and would return to this place of honor. This would be a good day to die, but a better day to make the others die.

"BROKEN LANCE, you and six warriors, go to the deep

draw that leads to the Sweetwater where the river is narrow," He motioned to the northwest, "You will see the dust of the wagons and when they near the river, you attack the Crow from upstream of crossing," commanded Red Pipe, chief of the Arapaho.

Lance was quick to select six men he knew as proven warriors and started to leave, but turned to Red Pipe to ask, "You will follow the wagons?"

"Yes, we will ride down Fish Creek beside wagons, until the Crow attack. Then we will move to attack. You will know when."

Lance nodded to his chief and motioned for the others to follow and they started just as the first gray light painted the sky overhead. Since the wagons had not yet crossed Fish Creek, Lance knew they would have ample time to reach the upper end of the Sweetwater long before the wagons made the crossing. He grinned at the thought of another battle, knowing this surprise attack would bring many honors for his warriors, and for him as a leader.

CHAPTER TWENTY
ATTACK

MORGAN AND WANNAMAKER SAT NEAR THE FIRE, SIPPING their hot coffee and staring at the flames, thinking about the coming fight and if there was anything else they need do to prepare. Morgan looked to Charley, "How 'bout you ridin' in back o' the last wagon with your Sharps. I'll have Smitty drive your wagon and with you at the back, won't nobody be shootin' at the wrong Injuns, an' if'n some o' them Crow try to sneak up behind us, why, you can take care of 'em with your Sharps. How's that sound?"

The old mountain man grinned through his tobacco stained whiskers and cackled, "That be fine, Cap'n. I can do that, yessirreee, but if the fight starts up front, I might have to hobble up thar to get in on it!"

"Long as there ain't no problems back there, then I'm sure you'll be welcome."

The old man cackled again as he rose to set aside his empty cup, picked up his Sharps and started to the designated wagon. He was heard to say, "Reckon I can get me a little nap 'fore everythin' starts."

Morgan and Wannamaker looked at one another and Morgan asked, "Where'd that big Whiskers get off to?"

"He done took off couple hours ago, said he was goin' back to them Arapahos, apparently he's married to one of 'em."

Morgan had instructed his people to make everything look as normal as possible, cookfires, eating their meal, packing up everything, all the activities of a typical morning. His concern was if there was an Indian scout, he didn't want them to know the wagon train expected anything. He rose and threw the dregs of his coffee at the coals and nodded his head to Wannamaker. "We'll be ready in 'bout a quarter hour."

Wannamaker stood, nodded his head to Morgan, and started toward his own wagons. As Morgan rode down the line, he spoke softly to each man at the reins. "Be sure to keep your woman and kids in the back and down as low as they can." He looked at each man to ensure he had his rifle and gear at the ready and moved on to the next wagon. Once he completed the line, he gigged his horse to a trot back to the head and seeing Wannamaker standing and waving, he waved back. With a twist in his stirrups, he looked back along the line of wagons, waved overhead and let out a loud, "Let 'em go!" The mules leaned into their traces, trace chains rattled, wheels groaned in protest, and the train began to move.

———

TATE MARKED the place where Bad Heart Bear lay behind the low rise, he was just behind that cluster of prickly pear below the top of the rise. Then he began searching the creek bed below to mark the whereabouts of the different warriors that would become his targets. One was hunkered down below the sharp edge of the creek bank by a large white stone. Another was using a dark-leafed kinnikinnick bush for cover. A third was stretched flat under the overhang of some willows. Others were farther down the draw, but these were enough for his first targets. Once everything started, there was no telling how long any of these would remain in place before charging the wagons.

He looked to his quiver to count the arrows and had a sudden idea. He looked again toward the low rise and chuckled to himself. *But, I can't do that til the wagons are near, just wanna scare him. Don't want him changing things, now they're all set, like we figgered.* He chuckled again and thought out his plan. He would use the bow for his first targets, not giving away his position, and then go to the Sharps. He crab-walked his way back from the top of the knoll. He had watched as the Crow took their places, and none had been behind him or near the knoll, so he believed he was out of sight for his preparations. Lobo also bellied his way to Tate's side and the man said, "We're gonna become spirits!" and began covering any exposed area of his attire and body with more alkali, and the same for Lobo.

———

WHISKERS RODE beside Red Pipe as the Arapaho started down the draw of Fish Creek. Just before them was the wagon trail as it dipped into the draw and up the opposite side and the first of the freighters was just dropping down to make the crossing of the creek. Whiskers stood in his stirrups and waved to Wannamaker who sat his horse beside the wagon and received a wave in return. Once all the wagons were across, the Arapaho would continue and ride the creek bottom as it paralleled the trail.

Red Pipe looked to Whiskers, "If we were not going after the Crow, I would want to take the wagons and all they have."

Whiskers chuckled at the man, understanding the temptation, and shook his head when he said, "I think we got 'nuff trouble chief. We don' need no more, at least not today."

Pipe grinned in agreement, and seeing the last wagon rise from the draw, he motioned to his men and gigged his mount forward to follow the creek bed and make their way to the anticipated attack.

———

BROKEN LANCE and his handful of warriors came to the mouth of the draw they used for cover to get to the upper end of the Sweetwater. He stopped the group and motioned for one warrior to scout ahead for any sign of the Crow. He looked to his left and the shoulder of a hill extended toward the river but also provided enough elevation he could see back towards the wagon trail. Motioning for the others to wait, Lance pointed his horse up the hill and soon crested the mound. Shading his eyes, he looked to the east for any sign of the wagons and saw a thin dust cloud rising about halfway between the bend of Fish Creek and the crossing of the Sweetwater.

He turned back to his men, motioned for them to join

him and they were followed atop the slight knoll by the scout. A young but proven warrior named Horse Killer, shook his head to indicate there was no sign of alarm in the valley of the Sweetwater. Lance had been thinking about the coming battle during the morning's journey and had determined the action to be taken. As they gathered on the knoll, he spoke to Horse Killer, "You and three others will go to the horse herd and drive them away but stay with them and we will share the herd when we return to our village. I will take the others and we will attack the Crow as they flee to find their horses." The other warriors looked to one another, pleased with the plan of Broken Lance, and eager for the battle.

TATE INCHED his way back atop the knoll, being certain to not show himself until he was ready. He slowly turned his head to look back along the wagon trail, saw the dust cloud of the approaching wagons, and turned back to pick his targets. While below the knob, he strung his bow and removed his usual floppy felt hat. Filling his hair with alkali, he believed his purpose was accomplished and he returned to the top where he now waited for the wagons to draw nearer.

Just below Tate's knob, Fish Creek made a sharp bend away from the trail, and back to run almost due west. This was where three Crow had taken their place of concealment below the edge of the bank and in the brush. But their position relative to the road made it necessary for them to face to the side to see the approaching wagons and Tate marked his targets. Tate knew by the positions of the attackers, their plan was to wait until the first wagon was near the last warrior before they sprang their trap, but Tate planned his time before the wagons reached the first.

He was tense and breathing deeply, readying himself as he watched the wagons draw closer and closer. Then he slowly rose to stand just back from to top of the knob but within sight of the warriors below, and he let his first arrow fly. While it sliced through the air to its target, Tate was bringing his second arrow to a full draw. Just before he let the string slip, he heard the thunk of his first arrow and knew it had hit flesh. The second arrow whispered away, and he nocked the third, his quick glance seeing the first target with only the fletching showing under his armpit and the body impaled on the arrow and held him to the creekbank, eyes and mouth wide, but unmoving. Tate's second arrow had also found its mark and the second warrior, having slightly turned when he heard the first strike, had slipped slightly down the bank resulting in the arrow taking him in the neck, killing him instantly. And not a sound was heard.

Tate stepped to the top of the knoll, leaned into his bow and brought the third arrow to full draw, lined it on the prickly pear cluster just below the top of the far rise, lifted it just a little and let it fly. He watched as the arrow arced over the wagon trail and disappeared behind the rise, causing a brief shout of alarm. Tate grinned, knowing that came from the leader of the Crow and Tate stood tall on the knoll and with Lobo as his partner, the two danced as if they were crazed Indian spirits, one a wolf, one a long dead warrior. He screamed and shouted as he had heard many of the Indians of different tribes do, and he waved his bow and flung his arms about, shouting screams that seemed to echo back from the low hills.

Tate saw the leader of the Crow standing, waving the black spirit arrow and shouting, just as the wagons came between the divided force. Tate saw Bear shouting to his men and the attack began, but belatedly and not with the force their leader had expected. A few of the warriors on his side had rifles, probably taken from the massacred at the earlier wagon attack and fired them at the first wagon and one warrior on the side where Tate danced fired his rifle, but none scored a hit. Arrows started flying and Bear was screaming at his warriors to attack, but as they rose, Tate saw them all looking his direction and back to their leader, but with Bear's shouts, they forced themselves to move from cover to attack the wagons.

WANNAMAKER HAD TIED his horse off to the back of the first wagon and now sat on the seat with the muleskinner. He was watching the rise to the right of the trail and letting the driver watch the creekbank. When Tate started his assault, Wannamaker didn't even see the man, and when he started his dancing and screaming, the freight boss was searching the nearby area for the source of the noise. He wasn't disappointed and when Bad Heart Bear stood and started his screaming and the others started shooting, Wannamaker dropped into the space between the seat and the toe board and brought up his rifle.

The two wagon bosses had agreed at the point of attack for the freighters to divide, three to a side, and wide enough apart for the Prairie Schooners to pull between the two rows. When the wagons began their move, the attackers were taken by surprise, causing them to pause in their assault. That instant gave the shooters in the freighters their opportunity to score a few hits on the raiders. When the schooners pulled to a stop, forming four rows of wagons, the settlers quickly dismounted and took cover behind the tall-sided freighters and with the freight crew shooting from above and the settlers from below, they soon turned the attackers back.

Suddenly the Arapaho rode up from the creek bottom beside the trail and took after the Crow, who were on foot and running for their horses. But most were quickly overtaken, and the Arapaho used war-clubs to drop the Crow in their flight. Both Tate and Bear watched the new attack. Tate immediately recognized the attacker as the Arapaho and was cheered by their arrival. Bear believed it was his people attacking the wagons, but when he recognized them as their enemy, the Arapaho, he screamed and lifted his rifle to shoot. The smoke from the fired rifle obscured the sight of Bear, but as it cleared Tate saw many Arapaho taking their quarry and dropping the attackers with wicked blows from their war-clubs.

The first to take flight from the attack were running toward the picketed horses beside the banks of the Sweet-water but around the bend from the confluence with Fish Creek. They had no sooner thought they would make it to their horses, when Broken Lance and his warriors struck at them with arrows and war-lances.

The people of the wagons stood and cheered when they saw the Arapaho attacking the Crow war party and went to one another, patting each other on the back and shaking hands and cheering the Arapaho. Tate dropped to one knee to watch, wanting to be certain that none of the

Crow escaped. He still heard screams and war cries as the attack continued, but the sounds moved downstream from his knob, so he slipped the bow over his back, picked up the Sharps that he hadn't even fired, and started down the slope to Shady with Lobo at his side.

There was brush at the base of the knoll and Tate used it as cover as he started toward the dry wash and Shady. Lobo whirled around and with teeth bared, growled. Tate also spun, bringing the rifle around as he did. A Crow warrior had come from the brush at the sound of someone near, and when he saw the white wolf, he froze in place and when Tate turned, the man screamed, shouted something in Crow and ran away, crashing through the brush and yelling. Tate looked at Lobo and said, "Are we that scary? He musta thought he'd seen a ghost!" He chuckled and added, "Maybe we better go dunk ourselves in the river 'fore we see anybody else, reckon?"

CHAPTER TWENTY-ONE
PURSUIT

TATE FOUND A SMALL POOL AT THE BEND OF FISH CREEK and lay back in it to let the cool water wash away the alkali. Lobo came bounding and splashing in beside him and the two friends cavorted like they had no care in the world. Tate stripped off his buckskins, scrubbed them together to get rid of the remaining alkali, and stepped back into them just as two women from the wagon train apparently in search of fresh water. He heard the women gasp as he turned around, slipping his tunic shirt over his head. He had already slipped his britches on and wasn't the slightest embarrassed as the women had hands to their mouths but continued staring at the broad-shoul-dered mountain man and his wolf pet standing in the middle of the only pool of water to be found on all of Fish Creek.

"Howdy ladies, pardon me a moment, an' I'll be outta here an' you can have it all to yourselves. By the way, you might not wanna get too far from your wagons, there's still some Indians on the loose!" He chuckled as he walked from the water, retrieved the reins on Shady and the three friends climbed up the riverbank to go to the wagons.

Morgan elbowed Wannamaker and the two looked at Tate as he approached. Morgan spoke up, "What'chu been doin', takin' a bath? You look more like a drowned rat than a mountain man!" Both men chuckled as did Tate and he looked beyond Wannamaker to see several blankets spread on the ground and covered with trade goods.

"What's that all about?" asked the wet Tate.

"We figgered we oughta show the Arapaho our thanks. That's all for them to pick an' choose as they like, or they can have it all. We got blankets, beads, geegaws, pots, knives, hatchets, we figger it's the least we can do," explained Wannamaker.

"Well, I'm sure Red Pipe and his men'll be happy to take that stuff off your hands. Course they'll have lots'a plunder off'n them dead Crow, and their horses too. But, they won't turn down what'chu got there. If you got some sugar, flour, salt, and lead, maybe some percussion caps, paper cartridges if you got any, muh wife'd be plum tickled to get some o' that."

Wannamaker grinned and said, "We can sure 'nuff fix you up with that. I'll get one o' the men to fetch it right away."

" I got sumpin' I gotta check on, I'll be back in a bit," answered Tate as he swung aboard Shady and started for the low rise above the roadway. He wanted to be certain that the leader of the Crow band had been taken; he knew his arrow had not killed him and he didn't want that man putting together another war party. He pushed the tail of his jacket back to have free access to his Colt Dragoon in the holster at his hip. With his hand resting on the butt of the pistol, he crested the low rise and began looking for sign. He found three bodies, already scalped and robbed by the Arapaho, but none that resembled what he had seen of the leader. He continued his search, following the tracks of the Arapaho that pursued the fleeing Crow, seeing a body now and then, but none that could be the man he thought to be the leader.

Tate saw Red Pipe and the big Whiskers talking as several of the warriors were busy loading some of the Crow ponies with their plunder. Tate rode up and the wide grin of Whiskers split his beard and the big man's voice boomed, "That went just like you figgered Tate!"

Red Pipe looked at the big man and then to Tate, "We planned good," emphasizing the 'we' so Whiskers would understand that Pipe was part of the planning.

Whiskers nodded his head, "Yup, we planned this thing right smart!" including himself.

Tate motioned to the men packing the horses, and said to Pipe, "You're gonna have more packin' to do. Them freighters and wagons got a bunch o' gifts laid out on some blankets for you. They're mighty grateful for you doin' what you did."

Pipe looked up at Tate who stood a couple inches taller and said, "Gifts?"

"Yup, blankets, pots, knives, lotsa things. Say, did either you fellas come across the leader o' this bunch? Big fella, bigger'n me, big top knot painted white, scalplock, bone breastplate, vest, braids with a couple feathers. He was by that ridge yonder above the wagons." He looked from Pipe to Whiskers, who looked to one another, then Pipe called Broken Lance over to ask him.

No one had seen him, but Lance said, "One man said war chief is Bad Heart Bear."

The name caused Pipe to look to his man and question, "Bear? I know him, and he was not one of the dead."

Tate scowled, looked at Whiskers and Pipe, "I need your best tracker to come take a look an' see where that sorry rascal got off to, can't let that one get away!"

Pipe sent Lance after another warrior and the two returned to go with Tate to the last place he had seen Bad Heart Bear. They topped out on the long low rise above the wagon trail and Tate pointed out to the tracker, Bear Claw, where the leader of the Crow was last seen. Claw dropped from his horse, examined the ground all around the spot. He began circling, investigating every track or semblance of one, then looked up to Tate, "He was here," pointing to the depression below the crest of the rise, "he moved much, then he and one other went that way," pointing towards the northwest and the western slope of the foothills of the Wind River mountains. "On foot, running."

Tate nodded his head and said, "I'm goin' after him and could use a good tracker if you'd wanna come along."

Bear Claw looked at the man known as Longbow and back towards Broken Lance. "I go." He reached for the dragging reins of his mount and swung aboard and looked at Tate as if waiting.

Tate grinned at the man, "Good. I need to talk to Red Pipe before we go." He motioned for Bear Claw to follow and he rode to the chief who stood beside Wannamaker, talking.

The freighter boss had a couple of his men picking up the remnants of the gift offering for the Indians and as

Tate rode up, "There's a man I been wantin' to talk to!" and stepped forward with hand extended to shake with Tate.

Tate slipped from his horse, greeted Wannamaker and turned to Red Pipe, "Chief, it 'pears as Bad Heart Bear and one o' his men got away. They're headin' up towards the west slope o' the Winds, and I'm goin' after 'em. Bear Claw's willin' to go with me, if that's alright with you."

Pipe looked at his warrior, a respected and proven man of the people, nodded his head to him and looked to Tate, "It is good. Bear Claw is good tracker and warrior."

Wannamaker spoke up, "Goin' after the one whut got away, are ye? Good, good. We're leavin' too. Got your horse packed with the stuff you wanted, no charge." Tate looked to see the dapple-gray he had traded from Whiskers and left behind with Red Pipe, loaded with a pack saddle and two panniers. "Gonna get a little closer to Fort Bridger and deliver some o' these goods. So, Tate, if you're ever in need, just go to Fort Bridger, us Mormons bought out Bridger, an' you'll allus be welcome! That what I tol' the chief here too. We'd like to trade with the Arapaho."

Tate looked from the freighter to the chief, nodded his head and stepped back aboard Shady, tipped his hat to the freighter and Pipe, and reined around to start his pursuit of the fleeing war chief of the Crow. The pace of a man and a horse at a walk are similar with the horse a bit faster. But when the gait is increased the advantage of the horse increases slightly. But a man can traverse and climb in areas that a horse cannot, while a horse has greater stamina than a man. Tate knew the Indians he pursued were experienced in the mountains and would choose trails that would limit the horses, so this chase would depend on his ability to out think the Crow leader.

The terrain before him was one of rolling hills but with many dry gulch ravines, rocky bluffs and ridges, scattered and sparse juniper, cedar, and pinyon, and a lot of sage, cacti and bunch grass. Tate yielded to Bear Claw and let him take the lead, following the moccasin tracks of the two Crow. They had gone just a short way when a voice behind him hollered, "Hey, wait up!" Tate turned to see the big mountain man with a face full of black whiskers astraddle a horse that looked too small for him, loping to catch up. He slid to a stop beside Tate and said, "I heard you was lookin' fer another fight an' I thought I might come along, if you was to have me."

Tate grinned at Whiskers and said, "It might be a long hunt," motioning to the far mountains.

Whiskers looked in the direction Tate nodded and answered, "Wal, dependin' on what way they go, that trail'll just take me closer to muh woman."

Tate chuckled, grinned at the man and said, "Come 'head on, then, glad to have the company."

Bear Claw had continued on his trek and Tate and Whiskers had to kick their horses up to a trot to catch up with the tracker. With the wide-open country, it was easy to ride side by side and the men talked, or rather Whiskers talked, and Tate listened, as they rode.

CHAPTER TWENTY-TWO
CHASE

TATE STOOD IN HIS STIRRUPS TO LOOK AHEAD ACROSS THE flats to get an idea of where the runners were headed. He pointed to the cut that marked the ravine that carried Fish Creek, and said to Whiskers, "Looks like they're goin' to the headwaters of Fish Creek. I figgered they'd swing around the southern end of the Winds and head fer home, but it looks like they're headin' fer the mountains."

Whiskers looked where Tate pointed and said, "If they keep goin', that'll take 'em to the headwaters o' East Sweetwater Creek, there's a trail that'll take 'em o'er them mountains an' down near that lake whar yo' cabin lies."

Tate's head snapped around and he looked at Whiskers, "Maybe he's lookin' for the rest o' his men, the one's we hit by the lake."

"Ummhumm, an' he'll be lookin' fer horses too."

As he took another look, he saw Bear Claw signaling and Tate said, "Let's go, Claw's got sumpin'." He dropped into his saddle and gigged his horse to a trot to catch up to Claw. The tracker was on the ground, pointing to the tracks, "Both have rifles," and he dropped to one knee to show the imprint of a rifle butt next to the tracks. "They stop here to rest, but soon on the run again. They move slower, tired."

"How far behind 'em, you think?" asked Tate.

Bear Claw lifted his eyes to the sun, extended his hands holding them flat and side to side, answered, "Three hands," the time it would take the sun to move the width of three hands across the sky.

Tate knew that to mean about two hours. He nodded and said, "Let's move, mebbe we can catch up to 'em 'fore they reach the black timber." The Indian nodded and swung back aboard his horse, reined him around and took to the trail to follow the runners with Tate and Whiskers close behind. The two Crow were now following the ravine of Fish Creek toward its headwaters but staying on the flats and rolling hills above the creek bottom. There was no trail they followed, but one was not necessary with their goal of the mountains and thicker timber in sight.

Another hour passed as Tate and company slowly followed the trail. Although there was no obvious attempt by the Crow to cover their trail, the terrain made the tracking difficult. Several times Bear Claw had to dismount and search for the tracks. Tate had purposefully kept Lobo by his side, but after the third time of losing the trail, he motioned the wolf forward in hopes of Lobo finding the trail. Bear Claw was walking beside his horse, searching for the sign, stopped and dropped to one knee and looked back to Tate. When the mountain man came to his side, Claw pointed to the tracks, "One went with the creek," and motioned with his hand upstream of the creek they had followed, "But one, maybe that way," and pointed toward the creek and the opposite bank.

They were near the headwaters of Fish Creek, the ravine that carried the water had widened and the stream became wider but shallower and the bottom of the wide swale was green with grass and flowers. The two runners had stayed in the dry flats before, but now the one that followed the stream went into the taller grasses to cut across the wide bottom. Tate dropped to the ground beside Bear Claw, looked at the moccasin tracks of the runners, and stood to look in both directions. To follow Fish Creek would take them to the headwaters and flat land with little cover, but if they continued in that direction they would soon find thicker timber as they came to the foothills. But to cross Fish Creek, there were several limestone formations and escarpments that would give good cover, and to continue that direction would take them to Pine Creek that flowed from the higher of the foothills, coming from deep within the black timber.

He looked to Claw and asked, "Can you tell which one?" pointing to the different trails and tracks.

"This one is bigger, heavier." He was still on one knee and indicated the track that pointed to the east and Pine Creek.

Tate looked to Whiskers, "How 'bout you an' Claw take that one," pointing to the track that continued to follow Fish Creek, "me'n Lobo will follow that one," pointing to the track that appeared to cross the creek and go toward the rocky hills.

"Alright, we can do that," answered Whiskers and lifted his eyes to the sun, shaded his bushy brows and added,

"It's gettin' on toward dark, shall we just keep goin' or you wanna meet somewhere?"

"I'm purty sure these two'll meet up somewhere, so let's stay on their trail. But, once it's comin' on dark, go 'head an' camp and make an early start in the mornin'. But keep one eye open, cuz they might try to circle back an' steal your horses."

Whiskers nodded his head and motioned to Claw. As they started on the trail once again, Whiskers turned back to see Tate and Lobo starting across the shallow waters of Fish Creek. As Tate and Shady rose from the stream bottom, they were faced with several limestone rock formations, escarpments that appeared to have been dropped randomly by the Creator. A few juniper and cedar dotted the terrain, but they appeared as solitary sentinels in the wide-open landscape. Lobo scanned the area, moving back and forth to pick up the scent of his quarry, looked back to Tate and up the slight slope toward a big knob of striped rock that stood as a mound that appeared to have pushed its way up from beneath the adobe desert soil. Several patches of rock, each appearing as wide swaths of weather smoothed stone, that allowed anything to traverse without leaving any sign of their passing were seen before them. Lobo started off on a slow lope, apparently having picked up the scent of the fleeing Indian. Tate squeezed with his knees to move Shady after the wolf.

After crossing a stretch of smooth flat rock, the sandy soil yielded tracks, but these tracks were going the opposite direction. Tate reined up and dropped to the ground to examine the clear moccasin marks. He looked at each track, and the trail seemed to go just the opposite direction, back towards Fish Creek. He stood, looked at Lobo who had stopped to wait for him, turned back the direction they just came from and knelt down again. He examined the sign closely, noticing the depression of the ball of the foot and the toes was deeper than the heel. This would normally indicate the subject was running, but the way the soil crumbled at the edge of the track, and the indentation that showed a push off told Tate that this man was walking backwards! But he hadn't counted on Lobo. The wolf didn't care what direction the tracks were pointed, he was following the scent, and it didn't lie. This man had moved in this direction, and the big wolf began pacing back and forth, anxious to be back on the track.

Tate looked at his friend, chuckled and said, "Good boy, he ain't foolin' you, is he?" He stepped into the stirrup, swung his leg over and motioned for Lobo to move out. Just before them was a slight mound with scattered limestone formations, a couple of trees, just enough for the trail to move in a wide swing to bypass the more difficult terrain and keep to the easier way around the mound. Just as the big rock mound came into view, the spang of a ricocheting bullet made Shady sidestep and drop his head as Tate dropped off the side of the horse away from the echoing shot, rifle in hand. Hunkered down, Tate ran to the limestone formation on the small knoll, Shady, the gray, and Lobo trailing close behind. He dropped behind the rockpile, turned to his back to catch his breath, and spoke to both Shady and Lobo, "You two were s'posed to see him first. What happened?"

He chuckled when he got no response from the animals, rolled over to his side and peered around the rocks. He was sure the shot came from the larger mound of solid rock, but he didn't want to expose himself to find out. He watched, waiting for any movement, and heard another shot that came from farther away, and he knew this must be the other Crow shooting at Whiskers and Bear Claw. *So that's it, they wanted to get us separated and maybe get one of us and take his horse. Well, at least this one missed, so far anyway.* He leaned away from his cover, trying to draw another shot so he could locate the shooter, quickly drew back, but no shot came. He looked around, spotted another rock formation, close to a lone tree, and decided to try for it. He took a deep breath, rolled to his knees, and slowly stood to a stooped over position, readying himself to run to the next cover. He lunged forward and did a zig zag move to get quickly to the other stone and heard nothing.

He dropped behind his new cover, waited until his breathing was even, and peeked around to see the big boulder. Nothing, no movement, no shot, nothing. But he decided to wait, because maybe that's exactly what the Indian wanted was for Tate to get impatient and move out away from cover, exposing himself to an easier shot. But Tate was patient, gathered some sticks for a small fire, and determined to put on some coffee.

He was sitting behind the knoll, enjoying his coffee, when he heard the approach of horses. He looked to see Whiskers and Bear Claw riding toward him, with Whiskers grinning as he smelled the coffee. When they drew near, Tate said, "I heard that shot, I was hopin' neither of you was hit, so I'm glad to see you're both still upright."

"Muh hat ain't," said Whiskers removing his dirty felt hat, sticking his finger through a hole in the crown and looking at Tate. "What 'bout'chu? Ya don't 'pear to be ventilated."

"Nah, just scared me is all. And I'm guessin' since he didn't shoot at you two, he musta lit out after he shot. That's prob'ly all they was tryin' to do, to slow us down a bit."

Whiskers stepped down and started toward the coffee, cup in hand, and nodded his head as he said, "That's whut I was thinkin' too."

Tate looked to the lowering sun, said, "This seems to be as good a place as any to make camp. Mebbe if they think they got us stopped, they'll hole up and with an early start tomorrow, maybe we can catch up to 'em. I assume the tracks you were followin' started this direction to join up with his friend, that right?"

"Ummhumm, 'peared that way. Prob'ly already joined up together. An' now they know we're follerin', we're gonna hafta be mighty careful."

"Yeah, I reckon. They'll probably take to a rougher route, makin' it hard for us to follow on horseback. But we'll just hafta take it one step at a time, reckon?" suggested Tate.

"Ummmhummm, now, how 'bout some o' that coffee," Whiskers asked, extending his cup toward the pot.

TATE WAS RESTLESS, FLIPPING THE BLANKET BACK TO LIE and stare at the stars, thinking, wondering, and fear began to creep beneath the covers of his mind. His family was just over those mountains behind them, and maybe in the path of the fleeing Crow leader and his companion. As Tate considered, he knew Bear planned the attack and since he was the planner, would have sent the other band of Crow up the Little Popo Agie to take the trail that would lead them down through the pines and to the Sweetwater River and the planned attack site on the wagons. And knowing his men had taken that route, but did not show up at the Sweetwater, then he would think something had happened to them or they were still in the valley of the Little Popo Agie. Tate knew the leader must be thinking about finding his other men or at least what happened to them and maybe get some horses and warriors to once again seek vengeance on the whites.

He rose from his blankets and rolled up his gear into the bedroll, walked to where Shady and the gray stood hipshot, and started rigging the gray. He looked to the sky, guessed it to be about two or three hours past midnight, but the waning moon still shone bright even at half. The sky was loaded with the stars and looked like God had spilled a bucket of diamonds on the black velvet canopy. As he swung the saddle on Shady, he dug out a couple strips of jerky from the saddle bags, stuck one in his pocket and one in his mouth, reached for the cinch and soon had Shady loaded and ready. He slipped the Sharps into the scabbard and was just starting to mount up when the gravelly voice of Whiskers stopped him, "Goin' some'eres?"

Tate turned to look at the big man that appeared as a mound like the ones below them, saw he was propped up on one elbow and answered, "I was gonna wake you, but I think I know where this renegade is headin'. I figger I might get ahead of him an' you two could foller his tracks just in case I ain't got him figgered right. Either way, one or both of us'll get him soon. If I'm thinkin' right, he's got one o' two ways to go. One, he's gonna foller this creek up to its headwaters an' cross o'er that ridge, then hit that trail some are callin' Sioux Pass. That'll take him down too near my cabin to suit me. The other way, he'll cross o'er this ridge," pointing to the timbered ridge east of their camp, "and foller it aroun' til he hits that trail we took from the lake over to the Sweetwater to hook up with them wagons. I believe he's lookin' for the rest of his war party, that bunch we done for when they attacked my family. Either way, he's pointin' himself too near my cabin and family to suit me, so I'd like to try to get there 'fore he does."

Whiskers stood and shook himself to wake up, "I was

kinda thinkin' the same thing, at least as far as them routes go." He looked up at the sky and to the black timber beyond, "It's still too dark to do any sensible trackin', but we'll sure be on their trail come first light."

"Good, I'm countin' on it." Tate turned to mount up, grabbed the lead rope of the gray, motioned for Lobo to take the trail and nodded to Whiskers as they rode into the dark. Tate knew this country, had hunted it many times, and ridden and walked these hills in the years spent building his cabin and living here with White Fawn. As he worked it over in his mind, he knew that horseback and walking would take different trails, and even though he was mounted, he might not make it to the cabin before Bear and his companion. But he must, one grave at that cabin was one too many.

He followed a game trail that rode the ups and downs of the run-off ravines that came from the granite topped peak to the east. They had camped on the lee side of a limestone topped knoll that stood away from the timbered foothills, with the creek trailing off to the south. He soon came to a fork in the creek, with the larger stream staying the course to the northwest. Tate pointed Shady to take to the knoll between the creeks and beyond a rocky shoulder before them. Once atop the wider butte, the moonlight showed the hillsides before him and the timbered slopes that held the many ravine runoffs.

He searched the draws and hillsides for any sign of fire or movement, not wanting to come upon the camp of the Crow unexpectedly. But there was nothing that gave away the location of the renegades. With the ridge of mountains to the east, he knew it would put him in the shadows until the sun crested the mountain tops, but he trusted the sure-footedness of Shady and the vigilance of Lobo.

The trail twisted about as it followed the easiest course that also provided cover, a tactic used by the animals of the wilderness to ensure their own safety. But it was not the most direct path nor especially the easiest. Just before entering the thicker timber, he stood in his stirrups and scanned the hillside by the light of the stars, and with his memory of the land and the dim light to show the way, he tried to put himself in the mind of the Crow to see what way they might choose to move. On foot, they would not be hindered by the need to take an easier route and could choose the steeper slopes and even the rocky topped ridges. He believed the Crow would purposely take a way that could not be followed on horseback, giving them the advantage.

He saw a saddle over the ridge, just south of the two taller peaks, that could easily be taken both on horseback and on foot, but he also knew the other side would be too steep for horses. Tate thought, *If I were afoot, that's where I'd go. A man on foot could pick a route off those steep escarpments and make it down the other side, where a horse couldn't.* As he gave it more thought he pictured the rest of the ridge that included the two higher peaks. Of those two peaks, one timber covered and the other with a lot of slide rock, he believed this crossing between the two was the only one this side of Sioux pass where he could cross with the horses.

He gigged Shady forward and they moved into the thicker timber as they followed the game trail above the creek bottom. It was a steady climb and the timber was thick, and opened into hillside parks, then the draw was filled with aspen and they moved through the white barked trees that shook their leaves at the passersby as if scolding them for entering their domain. The moonlight shone on the carcasses of several grey trees, long dead and bleached by the hot sun of long summer days. He knew this hillside had suffered a blowdown. It was not unusual in the mountains when the fierce winds of fall fight the coming winter and make an assault against the standing timber, resulting in a wide blowdown of all the trees that face the winds of wrath. These trees had fallen many years ago and were now obstacles in the way of new growth but would eventually be the fodder for the rodents that prowled the mountains and would be homes of grubs that would feed bears fattening for their long slumber of the winter months.

Tate broke from the aspen and mounted the ridge before him just as the sun was cresting the eastern mountains. He stepped down from the saddle, giving Shady and the gray a chance to get a couple mouths full of the grass and tundra tidbits as he surveyed the valley before him. This valley held the east fork of the Sweetwater and cradled the trail that would lead him over the Sioux Pass. He turned back to his mount, took the telescope from the saddle bags and took a seat on a large boulder before a tall ponderosa. He scanned the hillsides and the valley, looking for any movement that would be a giveaway of the runners. He saw a group of elk, pushed by a good-sized bull still in the velvet, moving down the draw, probably going to the greener valley below for a day of grazing. He saw a couple of black bear cubs playing tag as they shimmied up a big spruce, watched by their momma on the ground near a kinnikinnick bush. She seemed unconcerned and happy to feast on the bright red berries without having to share them with her cubs.

A small clearing showed magpies and ravens scrapping over some piece of carrion, probably the remains of a mule deer. Above it all circled a golden eagle with a wide wingspan that was multiplied when the sun cast its shadow to the earth below. An occasional shriek from the big bird could be heard as he used his clarion call to startle possible game into action, revealing their whereabouts. But nothing showed any intruders into the province of the wild beasts. After another scan, Tate stood and returned the scope to the saddle bags and mounted up to resume his journey.

As he swung aboard Shady he was thinking he had passed the runners in the darkness of early morning and he was now ahead of them on this trail. But if they started as early as did he, and if they took the steeper route, they could be well ahead of him. He shook his head at the thought and clucked Shady on the trail to pick up the pace in hopes of reaching the cabin soon.

WHISKERS SAT by the small fire waiting for the coffee, when Bear Claw rose and went to the trees. He poured himself a cup and stared into the flames, considering the day ahead, wondering where the trail might take them. When Bear Claw returned, Whiskers poured him a cup of the hot brew and the man sat down on a large rock opposite and lifted his eyes to the big man with a questioning look. Whiskers spoke, "He left couple hours ago, thinkin' he might get ahead of 'em. He wants us to follow their trail case they don't go the way he expects."

The Indian nodded his head in understanding, seeing no need to comment on the man's remarks, unlike most whites that seem to think they have to make some remark on every subject of discussion, whether they know anything about it or not. It was just a few moments later when the two were starting on the tracks of the runners, Bear Claw in the lead and often leaning down alongside the neck of his horse to check the tracks of the fleeing Crow.

The signs of the Crow led them on the trail alongside the creek below and showed the tracks of Tate and his pack horse as they followed in the night. But just as Whiskers was beginning to think of the two possibilities posed by Tate and that the Crow were probably moving toward Sioux Pass, the tracks faded and seemed to disappear. Bear Claw reined up and dropped to the ground. In the thicker timber, the trail was littered with pine needles and aspen leaves, making a carpet that made it difficult to find any sign of someone passing, especially from someone in moccasins. The tracks of Tate and the horses showed clearly where the many hooves stirred up the needles and leaves, sometimes striking the few rocks, but the tracks of moccasins did not show.

Bear Claw handed the reins of his horse to Whiskers, "I will search to see where they went," and quickly mounted the slope above the trail and began to scan the ground among the timber and scattered aspen for any fresh sign. Unsuccessful in his search, he went back down the trail until he found their tracks again. When they disappeared, he again moved to the uphill side to determine where they left the game trail.

Whiskers stepped off his horse to give the animal a

break from the heavy burden and to stretch his tree trunk legs while he waited. He listened to the sounds of the wilderness, grinning at the shriek of a red-tailed hawk, the song of a meadowlark, and the rat-a-tat of a red-headed woodpecker. These were comforting sounds to the mountain man, knowing that if there was any danger nearby, there would only be silence or at most the screams of alarms from different animals.

A short while later, a grinning Bear Claw came through the trees, gesturing to those above the trail and said, "They go up to cross over the ridge." He swung aboard his horse and gigged him forward to follow the tracks. Whiskers hurried up to get mounted and follow the tracker, knowing his horse had the more difficult job of carrying his bulk. But he was soon just behind the Arapaho tracker as they wove through the woods toward a cut in the mountains that would take them to the crest of the ridge. Whiskers thought, *Wal, Tate was right in his thinkin' that these Crow would wanna cross over, but he wasn't thinkin' they'd cross here. Wonder why he didn't think they'd cut o'er hereabouts?*

CHAPTER TWENTY-FOUR
HUNT

THE TRAIL TAKEN BY TATE KEPT TO THE SLOPE ABOVE THE creek in the bottom and pointed him toward the saddle on the ridge to the north. The shoulder holding the trail gave him a wide view of the valley below and he stood in his stirrups to pick landmarks for his descent.

Whiskers and Bear Claw were to follow the tracks of the runners, whichever way they went. Those tracks turned away from the creek bottom and started up a draw to the east and the ridge that came from the higher peaks at the tail end of the Wind River range. Bear Claw pointed his horse up the wide shoulder above the thick timber that cluttered the draw. The higher knoll gave a view of the string of timber that shielded the path of the Crow. That promontory enabled Bear to see the chosen route of the Crow and saw it would take them to the saddle notch just south of the smaller of three peaks. The southern two peaks were more intimidating and offered little passage, being covered with timber and rocky escarpments. A small park, devoid of timber, marked the notch that appeared to be an easy crossing of the ridge and the two trackers made their way through the thick timber littered with downed and bleached trunks, toward the saddle.

As they broke into the open park, the rising sun was blinding, and they shielded their eyes as they reined up and dropped from their horses. Bear Claw examined the tracks, looked in the direction they led and walked a short distance to the edge of the park to search below. With another examination of the tracks and shielding his eyes to look at the scene below and beyond, he turned back to Whiskers who had followed him. "They go through the timber, over that ridge and continue to that lake, there," pointing to the distant water that peeked from around the rocky ridge. The lake was probably five or six miles by line of sight, but they were on horseback and could not follow the runners through the rough country.

Bear Claw looked to Whiskers, "You take horses, I will follow them."

Whiskers looked to the Arapaho tracker, and asked, "You sure you wanna do this?"

"They are enemies of my people, they must die."

Whiskers looked in the direction the tracks pointed, then to the terrain below the park. He picked out his route with the horses, knowing it would take him back south before he could turn east and north to get to the trail that led to the lake. He guessed his route would cover close to fifteen miles and would not be easy going. He looked back to Claw, "Looks like I'll hafta go down that-away," pointing to the easier slope and timber covered ridges, "then I'll make it to the trail we took from the lake. I'm guessin' I should make it, oh, sometime after midday.

If you don't catch 'em 'fore I get there, you wait fer me at the lake."

Bear Claw nodded his head, returned to his horse for his small parfleche, and without another word, started on the tracks at a trot. Within moments, he dropped off the edge of the ridge and into the timber and was out of sight. Whiskers turned back to the horses, stepped aboard his big bay and snatched up the reins of Claw's horse and started off the ridge, leaning far back over the rump of his horse as he picked his way down the loose-soiled ridge.

TATE FOLLOWED the trail as it dropped off the ridge and into the finger valley that came from the towering granite top. Just below the peak, the mountain was marked with a wide swath of slide rock that pushed at the encroaching timber and kept it at bay. The trail was easy going, but he kept a watchful eye as traveling on it also made him an easy target. He had seen no sign of the Crow and did not know if they were ahead of him, or if he had passed them in the night. Either way, vigilance was necessary, and his head was on a swivel as he moved from the black timber to the openness of the white barked aspen. He crested another small finger ridge between two narrow ravines and paused to search the trees. He stepped down from the saddle and saw Lobo posed on a point of rock as he too searched the terrain. Without bothering with the scope, Tate sat on a rock and scanned the area. Below him, the wider aspen filled draw led to the creek beyond. Tate knew this was the east branch of the Sweetwater and the headwaters were just above this ridge, but below the saddle that held the Sioux Pass.

If the Crow had not crossed either of the possible saddles along the eastern ridge, this would be the best place to cross. And if there was no sign of their crossing, perhaps he was ahead of them and would make it to the cabin before them. With another quick scan of the draws and ridges below him, he mounted back up and started toward the draw with the aspen, knowing he would intersect the trail to Sioux Pass there.

He was getting anxious, and repeatedly gigged Shady as he climbed the trail to the saddle crossing of Sioux Pass. The Grulla dug deep, pushing himself up the steep incline, causing rocks to tumble behind and into the trees below. They zig-zagged across the face of the slope, working their way higher towards the crossing. Tate reined up, giving Shady a chance to catch his breath and him a chance to view the trail behind them for any sign of anyone coming up the slope. With no threat behind, he gigged Shady again to push up the last few yards to the crest.

Once atop it, a small park opened and offered low-growing, but green grass to tempt the two tired horses. Tate stepped down, loosened the girth on both, and walked to a rock outcropping to survey the land. Lobo walked beside the man and lay in the shade at the foot of the rocks. With scope in hand, he again searched for any movement that would tell of the fleeing Crow, but he was again disappointed and saw nothing. It was late morning, and any elk or deer or moose would be moving back into the shade of the trees to snooze through the heat of the day before coming back out in the cool of the evening to once again graze the mountain pastures. He did see an osprey circling overhead, watching the ground below for his daily meal. A couple of whiskey jacks sassed him from a nearby tree and a marmot scurried to the rocks after whistling his warning to any others nearby. But he saw no Indians.

He took the jerky from his pocket and began to chew as he looked in the distance to the lake by his cabin. He guessed it to be about three miles on the straight-away, but there was no trail through the steep-walled gorge that carried the creek from just below to feed the distant lake. He stood, stretched his legs, and dropped off the rocks to return to the horses. They were lazily grazing and appreciating every mouth full. Tate tossed the last of his jerky to Lobo and tightened the girths on the pack saddle and his own before mounting up to take to the trail again.

———

BAD HEART BEAR and his companion, Sharp Nose, were tired. Their trek had been, forced to cross the high ridge of the tail end of the Wind River Mountains, and then to work through the black timber. Their route had no obvious game trails and the downed timber slowed their progress. They tired early and had to stop to rest when Bear determined to follow a long finger ridge that took them to the well-used trail from the lake to South Pass. Sharp Nose looked at the tracks on the trail and spoke, "Many horses, are these from Pretty Eagle?"

Bear also examined the tracks and saw that a large group, easily the number that followed Pretty Eagle, had passed and the age of the tracks was about right. Bear nodded to Sharp Nose and said, "They passed here, but did not come to the Sweetwater."

"Should we follow to see where they went?" asked Sharp Nose.

"No, if they live, they will return. But I think they do not live," answered a stoic Bear. "We will backtrack them, return to our people."

"If we return with no bounty or captives, and all the warriors lost, we will return in shame," observed Sharp Nose.

Bear stared at the man, anger boiling in his eyes, and said, "We were betrayed! If Pretty Eagle had done as commanded, we would have been victorious! He betrayed us! It is not our shame to bear but that of Pretty Eagle!"

Sharp Nose dropped his eyes and looked down the trail toward the lake. He saw the whisper of smoke rising from the trees and pointed it out to Bear. "Maybe there are some of our people!" exclaimed the man, letting a slow grin paint his face.

Bear nodded as he looked, and answered, "We will see. But we must leave the trail and go through the trees. There may be more Arapaho or whites."

Sharp Nose nodded and picked out his route toward the smoke, Bear following. Within moments, Bad Heart Bear and Sharp Nose stood in the black timber and watched the clearing and the cabin below. Bear looked at the horses in the corral behind the house, pointed them out to Sharp Nose and said, "We will take the gray and one with black legs."

They started to move but when they saw a youth go to the corral and throw some hay from the lean-to to the horses, they paused, and waited. The young man stood for a moment to pet the gray, and then returned to the cabin.

Nose said, "We should wait to see if there are others," and looked to Bear for his approval.

The war leader grunted and stepped back into the trees to watch from the shadows, leaving Sharp Nose beside the tall spruce on the slope above the cabin. Nose saw movement behind the window, but nothing else. For several moments they watched and waited. The sunlight was streaming through the tall pines, showing shafts of light littered with the dust of the trees that danced. A camp robber jay, also known as a whiskey jack, scolded the intruders and bounced from limb to limb sagging of the fir.

"We go," ordered Bear as he stepped beside Nose. He pointed to the corral, "We will come from the trees behind the cabin, you go to the horses, I will stand back to see if someone comes. If the others still follow, we must do this quietly."

Nose looked to his war chief, nodded and started toward the corral. He moved silently through the trees, crossed the small trickle of a stream that passed below the grave and near the cabin, and in a low crouch, worked his way to the corral. Bear followed closely and just as silently, but when Nose went to the corral, Bear went to the back of the cabin. With no windows at the back, the only way they could be seen is if someone watched from the window on the stream side, but he saw no movement. Bear relaxed and leaned back against the log wall of the cabin, watching Nose catch the gray and put a bridle on the stallion. The man reached for the second bridle, hanging on the top rail when a voice came from beside the cabin and demanded, "Hold it right there!"

CHAPTER TWENTY-FIVE
TAKEN

SURPRISED BY THE SHOUTED ORDER, SHARP NOSE WHIRLED around and pulled his knife from the sheath at his waist and in one smooth movement as he started to drop into a crouch, raised the knife to throw at the target behind him. He was shocked to see a woman standing at the corner of the cabin, flaming red hair blowing in the breeze but with piercing eyes that showed no give. As he brought the knife over his shoulder the big rifle in the woman's hands spat smoke and thunder, and the .52 caliber slug tore through the man's chest, knocking him back against rail fence, to slide to a seating position, eyes wide but unseeing and unmoving.

Maggie gasped at what she'd done, but lowered the rifle to reload, dropping the lever and opening the breech. She reached for the remains of the paper cartridge and felt a sudden thud against the side of her head and her knees buckled and everything went black as she dropped in a heap, losing her grip on the rifle and bouncing off the side wall of the cabin.

When Bear heard the shouted command, he hugged the back wall and inched his way closer to the corner. He saw the barrel of a rifle protruding from the corner and he drew closer. Before he could reach, it roared and spat smoke and flame, startling Bear, making him step back. He saw the muzzle drop and knew the shooter would be focused on reloading. He quickly moved to the corner, tomahawk raised, stepped around and brought the flat side of the hawk against the shooter's head. The sight of the woman with the red hair made him hesitate but just a second before he struck out. Because of the shock of seeing her, he probably lessened the blow, but she went down at his feet, unmoving. He looked at her, nudged her with his foot, and turned to the corral. With two long strides, he made the pole fence and vaulted over, reaching for the reins on the gray. Once he had a grip on the reins, he went to the gate and kicked it open, swung aboard the gray and started to leave, but he looked back at the woman on the ground and hesitated.

He grinned and dropped to the ground, picked up the woman and draped her across the back of the gray, swung up behind her and dug heels into the horse's ribs and took off at a run, past the cabin and toward the lake. He was bound for the trail that followed the Little Popo Agie, the one his men were supposed to have taken before joining him at the Sweetwater. At least now he had a captive and his raid would yield some bounty. He wasted no thoughts on the death of the last warrior to follow him but searched the trees around for the war party under Pretty Eagle, but he saw nothing that would indicate they had returned this way.

. . .

TATE PUSHED DOWN from the crest of Sioux Pass all the while wishing he could go directly to the cabin, but the terrain disallowed that freedom. He followed the trail along the base of the back side of the tall granite tipped peak that was marked by slide rock that showed as a gray scar the length of the two mountains that stretched away from the saddle crossing. He knew this trail and knew it crossed two creeks before joining the one that led to South Pass, but he searched the terrain for any possible short-cut to the lower. When he cut through a notch that parted two timber topped hills, the first creek lay before him, but he stood in his stirrups, goaded Shady to the trees and the knob of a small hillock, and looked down the valley that carried the creek below.

He grinned when he determined this was what he was searching for and reined Shady around and back down to the trail. Once they cleared the timber and broke into the bottom of the small valley, he followed the stream bed due east, knowing it would come out on the preferred trail. He looked to the sun, guessed it to be nearing midday, and gigged Shady up to a trot. In a short while, they were on a slight slope overlooking the trail, and with one cursory glance, Tate pushed Shady down the slope to the trail below.

The sudden report of a rifle shot startled Tate, but without hesitation, he kicked Shady to a lope, dragging the gray behind. He was still about two or three miles from the cabin, and both horses stretched out and were soon in a dead run down the trail. As he neared the cabin, he reined up and moved into the trees; he had to see what the shooting was about before going charging into the clearing, that was a good way to get your head shot off.

He started to swing down, when he heard hoofbeats and saw the gray break from the trees toward the lake. There was no mistaking the top knot of the Crow war chief, but what was more alarming, was the bobbing red hair by his feet. His first thought was that the Indian had taken her scalp, but he saw her head bouncing and instantly knew it was Maggie belly down across the back of the steel dust gray and that Crow was taking off with her.

He dug heels to Shady and they bolted from the trees, but with the loaded dabble-gray in tow, he was slowed, but only momentarily. He reined up in the clearing before the cabin, "Sean! Sean!" he shouted. The door flew open and the tousle headed boy burst out shouting, "Pa, he took Ma!"

"I know son, I know. I'm goin' after 'em but I gotta get another horse first. Ever'body else alright?" he asked as he dropped down from the grulla. He looked expectantly at the boy and Sean answered, "Yeah, Pa. Ma shot one of 'em, he's in the corral, I saw him from the window and she went out to stop him, but we thought there was only one of 'em."

Tate started around the cabin, followed closely by Sean as the boy added, "Pa, he took my horse!"

Tate shook his head at the boy, vaulted the fence and caught up Maggie's buckskin, and with a strip of rawhide around her neck, led her from the corral. He grabbed a bridle and saddle from the tack shed, quickly saddled the mare and was starting around the cabin when he spoke to Sean, "Boy, I'm leavin' the gray here. You an' Ira strip him and put the goods away. But keep your rifle loaded and handy at all times, an' it'd be good if'n you all spent a little time prayin' 'bout it, too. But be careful, there's another

Arapaho comin' with Whiskers, you remember him, so don't go shootin' that one."

"You're gonna get her back, ain'tcha Pa?" pleaded the boy.

"I'm bringin' her back!"

Stripping the long lead from the gray and hooking it to the buckskin, Tate stepped back aboard Shady and reined around and left at a full gallop. He knew the trail the Indian was on and exactly where it led. He plotted it in his mind as he took to the shorter trail around the lake, whipping through the trees, leaning forward on the neck of Shady, mane slapping at his face as he encouraged his mount with soft words spoken in his ear. Lobo was a streak of gray flashing through the trees, not following the trail but taking the straightest course in his pursuit.

Bad Heart Bear kept the steeldust at a run as he followed the trail around the south bank of the lake. Downstream, the valley bottom was littered with bogs and brush, making him stay on the trail that followed the shoulder of the low hills on the south. When he came to the confluence of the outlet creek and the Little Popo Agie creek, he took to the trail alongside the Little Popo Agie. Now moving at a trot, the gray seemed glad to be on the move having spent the last week cooped up in the corral. Once they cleared the boggy flats, the creek took a sharp bend around a shoulder of the butte to the south, and the trail bent its way up and through a notch of the rimrock and rose to the top. Bear reined up and looked back on the trail to see if he was followed, but there was no one. He gigged the gray and started across the butte, knowing this trail would ride the rimrock ridges of the many buttes that followed the course of the river below. It wasn't an easy trail, but he would be able to see his back trail and make good time.

He placed his hand on the back of the woman, felt her breathing and knew she would be alright, hopefully he hadn't hit her so hard she wouldn't be in her right mind. He knew a woman once that had been beaten by her man and was never the same. Some said she had an evil spirit in her, and maybe she had for she had killed her man in his sleep not more than two moons after her beating. No one would have anything to do with her after that, and she eventually wandered off and died. He looked down at the mop of red hair and grinned; no one had a woman like this, most had never seen one. She was a prize indeed.

The gray trotted easy toward the bottom of the low slope from the crest of the butte and Bear pointed the stallion toward the trail as it crossed the little stream in the bottom. Once across, the trail bent to follow the bottom of the larger rimrock topped butte before them, working its way to the south east to bend around the lower shoulder before climbing to the top and back to the trail following the rimrock ridge high above the Little Popo River canyon. Maggie bounced on her stomach, uncomfortable, and in and out of consciousness.

CHAPTER TWENTY-SIX
PURSUIT

TATE CAUGHT A GLIMPSE OF THE CROW AS HE PUSHED THE gray up the narrow trail to the top of the butte. Tate pulled up behind the small hill that was the obstacle to the Little Popo Agie, making it bend back on itself but providing good cover for Tate and the two horses. While he waited just long enough for the Indian to resume his course, he stepped off Shady and mounted the Buckskin to give his Grulla a breather. Tate moved to the end of the hillock, looked up to the rimrock ridge and saw no sign of the grey horse and the kidnapper. He quickly started the mare around the bend and toward to trail to the top of the butte.

When he crested the butte, he saw the small dust trail of the Indian that showed his course to the foot of the bigger mesa, also marked by red escarpment that sat like a crown on the big mountain. Tate knew the trail would bend around the smaller shoulder and back to the crest of the mesa, but he also knew he could cut diagonally across the face and go through the notch between the two buttes.

If he could make it, he could intersect the trail of the Indian.

He kicked the Buckskin up to a ground eating lope, followed close by Shady and led by Lobo. He bottomed out and crossed the creek, pointing the horses at an angle across the face of the mesa, toward the notch in the rimrock. The lower part of the slope was easy going, but then he switched back and started the steeper climb. They moved at an angle toward the northwest across the steep slope, occasionally slipping and stumbling to catch their balance, but the horses labored on slowly. Whenever the Buckskin would stop, Tate gave it ample time for a breather and let it start out again of its own accord. Tate finally stepped down to lead the horses and turned back the other direction as they neared the rimrock. The hillside was so steep he often leaned down with his uphill arm to catch his balance to keep from tumbling down the slope. He picked his steps carefully, always aiming for the end of the rimrock and the roundabout trail that would take them to the top. The loose shale began to give him doubts about his choice, but he slowly moved, giving loose rein to the Buckskin and Shady, and one step at a time, several stumbles by both Tate and the horses, and he finally saw the shoulder of the rimrock and the trail around the point. He paused, breathed deeply, and looked ahead to see Lobo standing and looking back with an expression that said, "Hurry up!" Tate shook his head at the wolf and took a few more steps and finally topped the ridge, giving tension to the reins and stability to the Buckskin who followed close behind Tate and Shady just a few steps back.

Once atop, he dropped to a rock to rest, loosened the

girths on the horses for just a minute for them to blow and look for some grass, take a few bites and turned back, waiting. He breathed heavily, stretched to loosen some of the tense muscles, tightened the girths and turned with scope in hand, using the rump of the buckskin for a rest, and scanned the buttes and valleys beyond. Directly to the east, between him and another canyon with a creek beyond, was a basin of greenery. Across the basin, a trail was easily seen and at the north end, Tate picked up the movement of the Indian. He followed the gray with his scope, could barely tell that Maggie was still across the withers of the horse, and the Indian was following the trail that would take him along the rim of the Little Popo Agie canyon.

Tate quickly mounted up and kicked the Buckskin to a gallop off the butte and into the basin below. He turned to follow the trail and knew this would go between two smaller red buttes before bending back to follow the canyon. The Buckskin held a steady pace, moving across the basin without missing a step and gaining on the gray. The steeldust stallion was carrying the weight of two people and with the climb up the buttes and the distance already covered, even that valiant animal was tiring.

At the edge of the basin and before beginning the climb between the two red -ock buttes, Tate pulled Shady up alongside the Buckskin, and made the leap from one to the other. He dropped the reins of the Buckskin. These horses had been companions for several years and were as close as two could be, and Tate knew the buckskin would probably not even let Shady get out of her sight.

. . .

THE BOUNCING of the running stallion brought Maggie awake, but as her eyes fluttered open and she felt the taut muscles of the stallion against her bruised stomach, she knew enough not to make a cry or move. It quickly came back to her about shooting the would-be horse thief, the sudden blow to the side of her head and when she saw the fringed leggings and beaded moccasins of her captor, she realized she had been taken by another Indian.

She did her best to look around to see where she was, but the area was strange to her, the bald plains, the red rimrock; none of it was familiar. But she also knew she couldn't let this man take her away from her family. She had to do something. She tested her feet, felt no bonds, her arms hung beside her head and her hands were not tied, so the only thing that kept her on the horse was the man. She tried to see in the direction they were running, but she could only get quick glimpses, seeing nothing but a trail, rocks, and occasionally grassy slopes.

TATE KEPT his eyes on the dust cloud and the running steeldust stallion. He was laying low on the neck of his Grulla and his arms pumped with the motion of the horse's legs in the steady beat of the run. Lobo ran alongside, tongue lolling out, and he bounded over the flats. Tate looked down at the wolf, thinking *He's gotta be tired! How does he keep it up?* He looked ahead, saw the Indian pushing the gray beyond his limit, staying to the trail that mounted another red butte and climbed through a notch of the rimrock. Once atop the butte, the Indian reined up and turned back to check his back trail. This was the first time he saw his pursuer, and immediately reined the gray around and started again on the trail at a canter.

Tate saw the Indian turn, and spin away to again move to the trail. Tate knew he had to do something to slow the man and had a sudden idea. He pulled Shady to a sliding stop and quickly dismounted at a run. He had pulled the longbow from the sheath as he stepped down, strung it and nocked an arrow within seconds, leaned into the bow, and following the running gray, he moved the tip of the arrow well ahead and on the trail and let the black arrow fly. He watched for just a moment, saw the Indian slide his horse to a stop, and turn to look back at Tate. The Indian shook his fist in the air and kicked his horse again to take off.

MAGGIE FELT the horse stop and turn back. She carefully moved her head to look and saw only the red-rocks of the butte, and the horse was on the move again. Although not at a run, it still was hard on her stomach as she bounced with every step of the horse. Within moments, the horse came to a sudden stop, and the Indian turned and screamed as he shook his fist. Maggie realized she no longer had a hand on her, and she started to slide, but was grabbed by the man. She snatched at his leg, sunk her teeth into the buckskin leggings so hard she knew she drew blood and the man suddenly grabbed her leg and dumped her on her head. She grabbed at the ground, feeling herself sliding, and as she kicked and clawed she slid backwards and over the rimrock at the top of the canyon wall. The sudden sensation of falling and nothing to grab took her breath away and she was tumbling over and over, bouncing off the rocks and through the brush, falling down the steep slope and nothing to stop her descent.

THE INDIAN HAD to make an instantaneous decision when the woman bit his leg. He wanted to keep her, but the weight was slowing him down and the man behind was gaining. He quickly grabbed her leg, and threw her over, and without a look back, kicked the gray up to a run.

Tate was gaining, but he couldn't see the fleeing Indian for the dust cloud that followed, but Tate knew this trail and he knew that after the slight rise of the next red butte, the trail took a dip into a narrow draw and up the other side with a steep climb to the top. He kicked Shady as he leaned down and said, "That's where we'll get him boy, as he's climbin' outta that draw!"

Within moments, Tate saw the gray stumble as he climbed the low red butte, and knew he was getting tired. Shady hadn't faltered at all, even though it had been a long day for the horse, and they covered many miles and a lot of rough country, but this horse was used to these mountains and the thin air was like nectar to the Grulla and he seemed to bunch his muscles and pull for longer strides to overtake the gray. When they came to the edge of the butte, Tate brought the Grulla to a sliding stop and was on the ground before the horse ended his slide. With the Sharps in hand, he dropped to one knee and brought the muzzle down to get a sight on the gray, but he paused just an instant when he recognized Maggie was no longer aboard. He set the rear trigger, followed his target with the front blade and as the gray struggled to climb the far bank of the draw, the Sharps boomed. The roar filled the canyon, bounced off the walls and echoed back sounding as if an entire army had cut loose.

Tate watched as the Indian pulled against the reins, literally bending the neck of the gray back against his foot, and the two fell down the steep wall, tumbling over one another and coming to rest in the bottom. Tate jumped back aboard Shady, reloading on the fly, and slid down the valley wall with Shady digging in his heels and sliding on his rump. Once to the bottom, they quickly stepped out and drew up alongside the downed Indian and the gray. Tate stepped down from Shady and slowly walked to the Indian, watching for movement. When Tate neared, Lobo carefully walked beside him, head down, a low growl coming from deep within. Tate could tell the horse was dead, apparently with a broken neck as he fell down the slope. The Indian was pinned beneath the horse, with his chest and head showing. Tate started to reach out to the Indian with the muzzle of his rifle, but he saw his eyes flutter open. Bad Heart Bear lifted his head to look at Tate, grabbed for his knife but it was gone, reached to the other side for his tomahawk, but it too was missing. He scowled at the white man and turned wide eyes to Lobo as the wolf circled, growling and snarling, showing his teeth behind the curled lip. Bad Heart Bear struggled, and with a raspy voice forced from his almost crushed chest, asked, "Are you the one of the spirit arrows?"

Tate knew exactly what he was talking about but put on a blank expression and asked, "What spirit arrows?"

"The black arrows that came from the sky."

"Don't know nuthin' 'bout no arrows. But I do know you got some friends comin'," and he pointed to a couple of turkey buzzards already circling above. He had never known the birds to be that quick on the scene of death, but he wasn't going to argue with them.

The Indian looked to the sky and his eyes grew wide at the sight of the buzzards, a sign of evil to the Crow. He looked at the white man and back at the birds when Tate asked, "What did you do with my woman? The redhead."

The Indian snarled and growled, "I threw her off the ridge to the river below!"

Tate's heart skipped a beat and he glared at the Indian. He looked up at the buzzards and back at the Crow, the man responsible for the deaths of over thirty people of the wagon train, the man that personified evil and showed himself as a tool of Satan, the murderer of many others, and he said, "Those buzzards kinda take their time unless they see blood, so maybe I'll help 'em out."

He reached behind his back and pulled out his Bowie knife. He sat the rifle down on the rump of the gray, stepped beside the Crow and deftly avoided his outstretched arm, moved behind him and grabbed the white pompadour top-knot and pulled back on the greasy and matted hair, he said, "This is what you've done to many and will never do again," and ran the razor sharp blade around the top of his skull, cutting to the bone, and pulled hard on the repulsive handful of hair and scalped the man. The Indian screamed as Tate popped the hair from the top of his head, and stepped back, showed it to the Indian, blood dripping. What Tate held in his hands had been the pride and joy of the man, his distinguishing characteristic that made him stand out from the other warriors, identified him as Bad Heart Bear. Tate looked at the bloody scalp and tossed it aside, out of reach of the

Indian, but well within his sight. Lobo ran to the bloody mess, sniffed it and turned away to growl.

Tate went back to Shady, the Buckskin had followed Tate and Shady into the draw and now stood beside the Grulla, watching the man and the wolf. Tate mounted up and slipped the Sharps in the scabbard, looked at the Crow and said, "Now that they can see the blood, they won't take as long to come visit you." He waved at the Crow and took to the trail to retrace the man's steps and find his wife. With a shoulder lifting sigh, he looked to Heaven and asked, "Lord, I know that wasn't quite the way you'da done things, but," and he spat, "he was a mighty evil thing! Now, if you could forgive me for that, maybe you could help me find Maggie."

CHAPTER TWENTY-SEVEN
RETRIEVAL

TATE THOUGHT LONG AND HARD, TRYING TO FOCUS ON what he knew. And what he knew was he had to find Maggie and soon! If she had been thrown into the river as the Crow said, he might never find her, but he also knew the Crow would say anything to mislead him or at least to misdirect him. But until he knew, he had to search and that required every bit of his mind and spirit. *Now, where did I last see him with Maggie? Humm, she was there when he started up this last butte, and I shot the arrow just in front of him. She was on the horse before I shot the arrow, but when the horse reared up after he shook his fist at me, she was gone!* He kicked Shady to a trot, searching the ground for his arrow and any tracks or sign of Maggie. The trail followed the ridge above the canyon of the Little Popo Agie, in some places the rimrock showed and he saw a smattering of white rock, and asked himself, *Was it near that white rock?* He couldn't remember seeing the white rock before, but he had been watching the Crow and not the ground. He hung off the side of Shady, looking at the tracks, longing for a sign, any sign of where she might have fallen. Lobo stopped, and sniffed at the arrow, still impaled in the ground. Tate saw the shaft, lifted up and looked around. He jumped to the ground and started searching, "Lobo! Find Maggie! Find Maggie!" he motioned frantically toward the edge, looking for any mark, any disturbance of the soil.

Lobo trotted to the edge of the rocks, leaned out and looked down. Tate trotted along the edge, looking, hoping, wishing, and praying. "Lord, show me where she is!" he shouted to the Heavens. He looked to the ground, dropped to his knees and looked at the tundra, there, it looked like someone had been dragged, or slid or something. He crawled on hands and knees to the edge, Lobo came to his side and whimpered, looking below. At the edge, there was a sheer drop of about five feet, then a steep slope, littered with the debris, logs, new growth green sprouts, from an old forest fire, then another cliff face drop off, but as Tate leaned out as far as he could, he saw a shelf before another deeper drop off to the bottom of the canyon.

The shoulder appeared to stretch back along the face of the steep ridge and cliff, to his left, upstream of the river below. He stood and looked back along the ridge, to the shoulder below, and began running along the ridge, fearful but anxious to see any sign of Maggie, cloth, hair, even blood, anything! He ran, continually looking to the shelf and toward the end of the bluff. When he reached the point of the bluff, he mounted the cluster of limestone rock and scanned the shoulder, looking at every crevice, every rock, determined to miss nothing. A scar on the slope looked as if a trail led around the point of the bluff at the bottom of the ridge, and toward the shelf. Maybe this was the answer, a way to reach below the rimrock, maybe she was there.

He turned, whistled for the horses, and started running toward them. Tate, always the thinker and trainer, had taught his horses to come at his whistle, all for just such an instance as this when they were needed, and he had no time to chase them down. So, when he whistled now, they brought their heads up and started off at a canter to meet him. Without missing a step, Tate swung aboard Shady and they started at a run for the end of the bluff where he could take the trail and hopefully get to the shoulder below the rimrock. He was certain Maggie was there, among the debris and slide rock, and hopefully she was alright.

They dropped off the butte and followed the trail that paralleled the long stretch of rimrock at the top of the plateau. The hillside dropped away from the rimrock, holding many of the large chunks of the rock that time had worn away, and held them in abeyance of some act of nature that would send them plummeting to the valley floor. As they approached the big shoulder that marked the edge of the canyon, Tate pulled Shady up to a cautious walk. Hundreds of gray logs lay on the steep face of the slope looking like soldiers slain in battle, rocks broken from the rim were scattered among the dead trees and the trail abruptly ended as the slope became too steep to hold a trail. Tate jumped down and started on, climbing over the deadfall, clinging to brush, tree sprouts, rocks, anything to keep from plunging into the maw that waited and roared as the river cascaded over the rocks below.

He clawed his way across the steep slope and came to the shoulder he saw from above. The jagged cliff with the protruding stone that looked like so many monsters daring him to draw near, rose defiantly above him and stared at the rock pile and fire debris below that stretched out to the precipice of the canyon. But there, in the shade of the large protruding escarpment of limestone, a patch of yellowish brown that didn't belong. He ran, leaping logs, clawing over boulders, and approached the bundle of buckskin that lay unmoving in the shadows. He held his breath as he neared; it was Maggie. But her body was twisted, tangled in the brush and rocks, and there was blood, too much blood.

He dropped to his knees beside her and began to gently move her limbs, easing her to her back and moving the hair from her face. Her left arm was bent where it shouldn't be, her right leg was twisted about and appeared to be broken. Her buckskin tunic and leggings were ripped, torn, shredded. She had cuts and scratches on her arms, legs, and face, and several welts and bruises on her face, shoulder, and limbs. But her eyes fluttered, and she breathed. Tate finally caught his breath and asked softly, "Maggie, Maggie?"

She muttered, mumbled something incoherent, tried to move, winced and scowled and tears chased the dirt down her cheeks.

Tate said again, "Maggie, it's me, Tate. I'm gonna get you home, but it's gonna hurt a bit, you're in a pretty bad spot and a pretty bad way, but don't worry, I'll get you home. I promise."

Her eyes fluttered again, and she murmured, "Home,

home, love," and the words dwindled to less than a whisper and her breathing was shallow.

Tate folded her arms across her chest, bent beside her and with an arm under her shoulders and the other under her knees, he carefully picked her up and started back. Every step was calculated, carefully placed, as he moved cautiously across the narrow shoulder. The cliff rising to his left, and the canyon threatening to his right below. He took a step, tested it, shifted his weight, fearful the ground would slip from under his feet, and then took another. When he came to the steep stretch with all the debris, he lifted her to his right shoulder and slowed his pace, having to be extra careful, one slip and he could lose her, or both could disappear into the canyon. But he held to her tightly, even when crawling over a log or more, he refused to loosen his grip, and with his eyes on the waiting horses, he finally cleared the last hurdle.

He carefully lifted her to the saddle and climbed up behind her. He held her close against his chest and reined Shady around to start for the cabin. With each step and creak of the saddle, Maggie winced or groaned, but they continued.

Twilight winked through the trees below the cabin as Tate pointed Shady to the clearing. He stopped below the porch and started to step down, but was stopped when Whiskers came from the cabin, with Sean and the others close behind. No one spoke, but all looked at Maggie, mouths open, hurt showing in their eyes, and Whiskers reached up to help Tate lower Maggie from the saddle. The big man cradled her in his arms and Tate mounted the steps and motioned the others aside as he pushed open the door and led the way to the bedroom and their bed. Whiskers carefully lay her down, treating her as a fragile piece of fine china.

"Vicky, could you put some water on the stove please, and get me some o' them dish towels of your ma's. Sean, you and Ira, could you put the horses up?"

Sadie stood quietly beside the bed, looking at her mother, fear showing in her eyes, "Daddy, will Momma be alright?"

"Yes, baby, but it's gonna take all of us helpin' and doin' ever'thing we can."

Whiskers stood in the doorway watching, and with a sudden idea, he blurted, "I'm gonna go get muh woman, Red Hawk, she knows 'bout these things. She's got all them herbs an' plants an' such, I can fetch her an' be back come mornin'!"

Tate turned to look at his friend, saw Bear Claw behind him, and said, "Whiskers, I'd appreciate that, sure would. She," nodding toward Maggie, "needs all the help she can get. I'm gonna hafta splint her arm an' leg, but it might wait til Red Hawk gets here. I'll do what I can, but she does need a woman an' somebody whut knows more'n me."

The big man nodded, turned on his heel and pushed Bear Claw aside and the two went to the door and were on the trail within moments. Tate turned back to Maggie, took a couple of the small towels from Vicky and started cleaning the cuts and scrapes. "Vicky, Maggie's got a pouch o' stuff over there in the corner. There's stuff in there for a poultice an such, so, if'n you can get one o' them bowls an' put some hot water in it, then the stuff in that little satchel, and make a paste, then we can use it on these bad cuts."

Vicky did as asked, and soon had the poultice formed and ready for Tate to apply. He continued to shake his head at the many cuts and abrasions as he cleaned the wounds and quietly muttered a prayer for God's guidance and healing touch.

CHAPTER TWENTY-EIGHT
HELP

MAGGIE STRUGGLED, TRYING TO COME FULL AWAKE, BUT every breath, every move brought additional pain. She tried to twist to a more comfortable position, but the pain drove her back into the refuge of unconsciousness. Tate examined the broken arm; it appeared to be a simple break half-way between the wrist and the elbow and was not too far out of place. He looked to the leg and it bent at the knee and again just below the knee. He had set broken bones before, but with the help of others to hold the patient and stabilize the break. He examined the rest of her body, saw what appeared to be at least two broken ribs, maybe more, and the sizable bump on her head was of concern as well. He dug through Maggie's bag of medicinal supplies and was relieved to find the pouches all labeled. But the bag with willow bark was almost empty and he called for his son, "Hey Sean, I need you an' Ira to go fetch me some willow branches. Get a good arm load from down at the stream below the trail."

"Sure Pa," answered Sean, pleased at being able to help.

He and the others had paced from the porch to the table, whispering to one another, none having any answers. Now that he could actually do something, a grin stretched his face as he grabbed his hat from the peg, snatched up his rifle by the door and tossed a bag to his friend and followed Ira out the door.

Tate turned to Vicky, "We're gonna need some more hot water. We'll need to make some more poultices and some tea. So, if you could put a pot on the stove, that'd be a big help."

"Sure, glad to help," answered the girl as she took the pot from the stove, added several ladles full from the wooden water bucket, and put it on the stove. She used the lid lifter to check the coals, added a couple of pieces of wood to rekindle the fire and replaced the cook lid.

She returned to the bedroom to see if there was anything else she could do, and Tate explained, "When the boys get back with the willow, we'll need to peel the branches and get the inner bark. We'll put a few leaves with it and steep it in the hot water to make a tea for Maggie. Then we'll use the rest to make some poultices for the pain on her leg and arm, and for the bad cuts. It's kind of a medicine for pain, and she needs to get some rest."

"But what about her leg and her arm?"

"Well, they're broken all right, but it's gonna take some doin' to get 'em set. It takes someone to hold her tight and unmoving, and I'll have to put a lot of pressure on her arm, pulling it straight to get the bones lined up proper, and then we'll splint it and bandage it tight. Same with the leg."

"Can I help?" asked Vicky, showing her concern for the woman she saw as a mother figure.

Tate looked at the girl, back at Vicky and thought a moment, knowing it would be best to get the bones set as soon as possible, and it would be easier to do it while she was still unconscious, but his concern was if Vicky or Ira or both would be able to hold Maggie still while he worked. He lifted his eyes to the girl, "Let me consider it, Vicky, I know you want to help, but whenever we do it, we can't make any mistakes and make it worse. Let's get the willow tea down her and the poultices on and see how she does. We might have to give it a try, but let's just wait a little."

Vicky nodded her head and returned to the stove to check on the water. The boys came in, each with an armload of willow branches and laid them on the floor by the table. Sean grabbed up one and went into the bedroom to get instructions from Tate.

"How's she doin' Pa?"

"Well, she's in a lot of pain, but that's why you got the willow. Here, let me show you what to do." He took the branch from his son, stripped off the small branches and with the tip of his big Bowie, he split the bark the length of the branch. Then he began to peel the bark away and said, "Keep the bark, put it in a pile on the porch, then take your knife and scrape off this inner layer of thin bark. After you get a couple hands full, take the water pot off the stove and put the strippings in the pot and maybe a handful of willow leaves, the dryer ones, and let them steep for a while, until the water shows a bit of color. Then have Vicky bring a cup of that tea in here for your ma."

"Alright Pa, we'll get right to it."

EVEN AFTER GETTING a little over a cup of tea down her and having rolled up blankets to stabilize her leg and arm, Maggie still struggled. She was restless and in pain and there seemed to be no relief. Her breathing was ragged, and each deep breath brought moans of pain, probably due to the broken ribs. Tate rose from the chair by the bed, yielding his seat to Vicky and picking up the lantern from the table, he spoke to the boys, "You come out with me, I need one of you to hold the lantern and the other to stand ready with a rifle. I'm gonna split some wood to make some splints, then we'll hafta work at settin' Maggie's breaks." The boys nodded, grabbed their hats and the rifle and started out the door after Tate.

Choosing a smaller straight dry log, Tate cut it to length, then split two slabs the length of the log. After inspecting them closely, he used the blade of the axe to trim it up and smooth it as much as possible, then split an additional slab, cut it in half and smoothed it as well. Satisfied, he walked back to the cabin, followed by the boys.

Once inside, he rummaged in the bedroom for an old pair of leggings, and used them to wrap the splints, trying to make them as comfortable as possible. He looked at his craft, breathed deep and looked at the youngsters, who were watching him expectantly. He began, "Alright, here's what we're gonna be doin' . . . " and proceeded to explain in detail what would be necessary and what each one would be expected to do. "Now, everybody understand?" Each one nodded, looking to Tate and to one another, wide-eyed and a little fearful. He had told them she might cry out, maybe even scream, but they could not let go or let her move.

When he stepped to the side of the bed, he gently lifted her head and shoulders, removed the pillows from beneath her and lay her back flat on the bed, adjusting the ticking and feathers to be as stable as possible. "Vicky, you slip up there beside her, be ready to hold her head in your lap and maybe hold on to her other shoulder. Sean, you sit there by her shoulder and you hold on to this shoulder and her upper arm. I will probably put my foot in her armpit when I have to pull, so be ready. Ira, you hold the splint here, and be ready with them strips of buckskin to tie it down." He looked at each one, asked, "Everybody ready?" He looked from one nodding head to the other, took a deep breath and picked up Maggie's hand, grasped her wrist with both hands, and with his left moccasined foot in her armpit, he started pulling to straighten the arm.

It went surprisingly easy as he stretched the malformed arm straight, and with the tension kept by one hand, he felt along the arm with the other, and satisfied, nodded to Ira to place the splint as he had instructed. During the setting, Maggie had moaned, but didn't resist, still breathing a little raggedly, but she appeared to take a deep breath once the splint was in place and bound tightly. Tate took over the wrapping of the splint, using long wide strips of buckskin, held and handed to him by Sadie, and wrapped the entire splint and stabilized her hand and wrist as well.

Tate sat back, looked at the youngsters and said, "Good job. You did very well. But now, the leg is going to be a bit more difficult. Vicky, you and Sean stay where you are, but this time you'll have to have a good grip on her shoulders. Ira, you'll need to be ready to stabilize her knee and the part of her leg just below it. Once we get it set, then be ready with the slab that will be on the inside of the leg, and Sadie, you hold that other slab for Ira." Tate looked at Maggie; her eyes fluttering and a slight moan slipping from her lips, but still unconscious. He took another deep breath and started.

It took three tries, and Vicky had to lay across Maggie's middle, away from the ribs, and help keep her torso straight while Ira maneuvered the leg below the knee. Tate provided the tension to pull the leg straight, but with greater muscle in her leg, it was difficult to get the break aligned satisfactorily. But on the third try, and a few stifled screams from Maggie, success. With the buckskin wrapped splints in place and tightly wrapped with wider strips of the soft leather, Tate was satisfied with their work. Maggie seemed to be a little bit relaxed, and with a little more pain-relieving tea taken in, she lay still and rested more deeply than before.

THE SUN STARED through the pines and pierced the window to bring Tate awake. He had fallen asleep, chin on his chest, in Maggie's rocking chair beside the bed. He opened his eyes to see Maggie looking at him, wrinkles maring her brow, as she tried to force a smile. Between ragged breaths, she said, "Remind me . . . not to go . . . to sleep on you again. Don' wanna get...wrapped an' strapped like this."

Tate chuckled at his courageous bride and answered,

"Had to do sumpin' to keep you still! You were talkin' 'bout wantin' to do all sorts o' things, none of which made any sense by the way, so you're lucky I didn't tie you down!"

"What happ...ened?" she looked at him, frowning.

"Well, after you killed one Injun, another took off with you and threw you over a cliff, that's all, you know, a usual day in the mountains."

"Why'd he...throw me...over a cliff?"

"I think it had sumpin' to do with you bitin' him."

"Oh, that all?"

"Ummhumm, but don't go tryin' it with me. Won't work. I'll just turn you over my knee and give you a spankin'!" He tried to keep a serious expression, but the relief of the moment tugged at the corners of his mouth and his eyes were alight with love.

Maggie started to laugh, winced, held her middle, and shook her head for Tate to not do that again.

It was a relief to see his wife awake and talking, but he knew it was going to be a long time recovering. However, he knew his woman was as tough as they come, and he was confident she would be up and about soon. He spoke a silent prayer of thanks and smiled at his bride.

CHAPTER TWENTY-NINE
CONSIDERATION

TATE WAS A WELL-EXPERIENCED AND QUITE GOOD COOK, AS long as the cooking was done over a campfire and in a skillet. But now he poked through things on the shelves above and below the counter, trying to find his way in this foreign land that was usually inhabited by women. Or at least by one woman, Maggie. Vicky and Ira sat at the table, watching Tate, and she was giggling at his antics and obvious frustration. Vicky stood and went to his side and said, "How 'bout you let me take care of things here, you can go, oh, chop wood or something more suited to your talents."

Tate looked at the girl, surprised but relieved, and turned away as he said, "You sure you don't mind?"

"No, of course not. My ma taught me a lot about cookin' and such; I'll be fine. You two go on now, and I'll call you when breakfast is ready. Take your coffee with you," she added as she motioned to the steaming cup on the table. "Sean and Sadie are outside with Lobo, so if nothing else, you two can keep an eye on them," and she lowered her voice as she said, "or vice-versa." She looked up and grinned at the two as they started for the door.

She took down a bowl and started mixing up some biscuit dough, greased the dutch oven and went to the fireplace to pull out some coals to heat the cast iron. Returning to the bowl, she blended the flour, water, and sourdough as she prepared the biscuits. She rolled out the dough, grabbed the biscuit cutter and cut out several and sat them aside, rolled the dough once again and cut the remainder. Putting the raw cut dough on a plate, she went to the fire, knelt down beside the now hot dutch oven, used the lid lifter to set the lid aside and arranged the biscuits on the bottom, put in the three-legged stand, added more biscuits and replaced the lid. With the coal shovel, she added a couple of scoops to the lid, checked the coals on the bottom, and satisfied, returned to the counter.

Vicky hummed a familiar tune she remembered from the little country church her family used to attend, called "My Mother's Bible." As she hummed and remembered the words, her eyes overflowed, and tears streamed down her cheeks.

This book is all that's left me now. Tears will unbidden start!
With faltering lip and throbbing brow, I press it to my heart,
For many generations passed Here is our Family tree;
My Mother's hands this Bible clasped, She dying gave it me.
My Mother's hands this Bible clasped, She dying gave it me.

She sat down at the table and with face in her hands, she wept. Since the time of the Indian attack and losing her family, she had not freely mourned, and it came like a flood, her shoulders shaking and tears dropping to the table. She reached for the dish towel on the table and wiped her face, took several deep breaths and stood to return to the counter. She busily worked, but still she hummed, and she basked in the memories of home and family, remembering times spent with her mother as they prepared meals for the family. She dredged the strips of venison steak through the flour, took them to the skillet waiting on the rack above the fire. Before long, the fried steak, gravy, and biscuits were ready, and she went to the door to call the family. As she waited on the rest, she dished up a plate for Maggie and took it to her.

Maggie waved her off and said, "I don't feel like eating, but maybe I'll have a biscuit later," and she forced a weak smile.

"Whenever you're ready, I'll bring you what you need. You just rest," advised Vicky as she looked at the frail figure on the bed.

Maggie grinned, and answered, "Yes, Mother."

Vicky giggled and turned away to return to the table and the rest of the family. She sat the plate of meat beside the basket of biscuits and the bowl of gravy. Everyone took a seat and Tate had them hold hands as he prayed for Maggie, the meal, and the family. When he finished, everyone said "Amen" and they began their feast.

When they were still busy, Tate was dishing himself a second helping of gravy over a biscuit, he asked, "So, I know I haven't been around much since we brought you two here to the cabin, but have you thought much about what you want to do?"

"Whaddya mean?" asked Ira, between bites of fried steak.

"Wal, you know, with your lives, I mean. I'm sure that before the attack on the wagons, you weren't plannin' on livin' in the woods with a bunch o' strangers, fightin' off Indians, were ya?"

Vicky giggled at the expression and then with a more serious expression, "We've talked a little, but we really don't know what we could do. Our folks had things all planned out, you know, goin' to Oregon and startin' another farm. Both our families were farmers, and I guess we were expected to be farmers too."

Ira spoke up, "There's a lotta things I thought about 'fore the attack, but now, I don't rightly see how anything like that's possible."

"What kinda things?" asked Tate.

"Oh, you know, the kind of work or trade I'd like to do, something workin' with my hands, like a blacksmith or somethin' like that. Farming's alright, but it takes a lot to get your own place, and some o' the trades let ya apprentice with 'em, you know."

"Yeah, they do. There are a lot of things like that in the cities. But it is hard to get a start, especially when you don't have family to help. What about you, Vicky, what have you thought about?"

She dropped her head, her cheeks and neck showing a touch of red as she felt a little embarrassed. "The only thing I've ever wanted to do was to be a wife and mother. I don't think there's anything more special than that!" She lifted her head and tried not to look at anyone as she poked at the food on her plate.

Tate looked from Vicky to Ira and thought about their ages. Many young people their age would be getting married, some even earlier. But that was only when the young man had a trade or some way of supporting his family. Both of the young people were staring at their plates, and Tate began to realize they had thought about just that.

"Well, there's something I should tell you. Maybe I should have said something to you before, but when I met up with that other wagon train, I asked if there was anybody travelin' with 'em that wanted a family but didn't have one. The wagonmaster said there was a couple that lost their only child and were wishin' they had other children. Now, he was gonna talk to 'em about the possibility of fillin' in as your ma and pa, but I don't know if that'll happen. The wagon train was gonna rest their animals and such for a few day, but I don't know any more than that.

"Also, if somethin' like that didn't suit ya, Maggie and I are willin' to do anything we can for you to make a life for yourselves. Don't know what that'd be exactly, but we'll help all we can."

Ira looked up and asked, "You mean, like if we wanted to live in the woods, like you do?"

"Wal, I suppose that'd be a possibility. But there's other things. There are some tradin' posts like Bridger's, and Bent's, that sometimes take on help. Or it might be to get you a way back east with some freighters. You got any family left back there?"

Ira answered, "No, I don't have any family, and all Vicky has is an old maid Aunt in St. Louis. We talked about going back, but I don't know what we'd do, or how."

Vicky looked up at Tate and back to Ira, "We also talked about starting life together, you know, get married and all, but what would we do? I don't know if we could make it in the mountains like you and Maggie."

Tate grinned as he looked at the two, "I think that's

fine, yes, mighty fine. But, two things that are important for you to consider. One, you're still young and you don't have to do anything just because you think it's time or anything like that. And two, something you need to be sure of, is do you know the Lord as your Savior?"

Both the young people looked up at Tate, somewhat surprised at the question and Vicky responded, "Uh, yes, of course. My family was always in church and I accepted Jesus as my Savior when I was much younger. But why do you ask that?"

Tate chuckled and answered, "Well, I could probably preach about that a little, but it's just this simple, if you're both not going the same way, eventually the roads you're traveling will take you in different directions. But, if you both have Christ in your lives, then you'll travel the same road to the same location and it makes life together so much better. So, how 'bout you, Ira?"

"Yessir, my ma was pretty strict about those things and when she tucked us boys into bed ever' night, she'd kneel by the bed and pray for us and ask Jesus to work in our lives until we accepted Him. So, when I finally under-stood what it meant to do that, I prayed with my Ma and asked Jesus to forgive me of my sins and come into my life and save me, and He did!"

Tate grinned and patted Ira on the back, then spoke to both, "There's no hurry about any decision, and if you have any concerns, or questions, I'll do my best to answer. So, I'm gonna check on my wife, and you and these other two," looking at Sean and Sadie who had sat listening to everything, "can clean up the dishes and such."

. . .

As he stepped through the doorway, Tate saw Maggie resting peacefully, and he moved to tuck the blanket around her and cover her exposed, splinted leg. The window was open to give plenty of fresh air and Tate tiptoed out, pulling the door closed quietly and started for the door. He saw the four youngsters working in harmony as they cleared the table and stacked the dishes. Ira picked up the water bucket to retrieve more for the cleaning chore and followed Tate out the door. Tate had no sooner seated himself on the porch, when he heard the clatter of hooves from the trail below the clearing. He stood, picked up his nearby Sharps, and stepped to the top of the stairs to see who was coming.

Red Hawk, astride a colorful paint horse, led the two into the clearing, with a wide smile that showed her happiness at returning to see Maggie. But her concern was also evident as she quickly dropped from the mount and grabbed her large beaded bag and started for the cabin. Tate said, "Howdy Red Hawk,"

Before he could continue, she asked, "How is she?"

"Well, right now, she's resting. But we had to splint her leg and her arm, bandaged some o' the other injuries, but she needs more. I know she's got a couple broken ribs, and probably more, but I'll let you take care of all that." He opened the door for her and pointing her to the bedroom, stepped back on the porch to greet Whiskers. He grinned at the big man and walked down the steps and said, "Thanks Whiskers! You know where to put the horses, but I'll help you."

"So, how's she doin'?" asked the big man as they walked around the house to the corral.

"She's in a lotta pain. Broke leg, broke arm, couple ribs,

lotsa cuts, took a good lick on the head. Had it been a lesser woman, it'd killed her. But Maggie, she's tough, thank the Lord."

Whiskers turned to look at the man when he mentioned the Lord, then continued on to the corral. "Wal, we're prepared to be here as long as it takes. Muh woman kinda took to your Maggie when they met b'fore, an' she wants to do ever'thing she can to get her better. She knows what she's doin' too, she studied with a Shaman fer a couple years 'fore I come along an' swep' her off her feet!" he chuckled at the memory.

"You're mighty welcome, and I'm thankin' you for comin'," answered Tate, his relief evident.

CHAPTER THIRTY

COMPANY

"Yassuh, Cap'n, you sent fer me?" asked the old timer
called Charley. He had come from his wagon when Smitty
the scout told him the wagonmaster was asking for him.
The wagons had moved a couple of miles upstream and
across the Sweetwater, wanting to get away from the
scene of the battle and the many carrion eaters that had
descended upon the area. But the people and the animals
were in need of a rest and it had been a long climb and
several days since they had taken the time to work on the
repairs of the wagons. Morgan, the wagonmaster had
suggested now would be a good time for a three or four-
day break to restore their larders of meat and make any
needed repairs.

When Charley arrived at the wagon where Morgan
waited, he was wondering just what it was the man
needed of him.

"Charley, you remember the Johnstons, don't you?"
asked Morgan.

Charley nodded to the couple seated on a bench made

from a board and a couple of trunks beside the wagon. They were a reasonably young, probably around 30, guessed Charley, and a handsome couple. But the man was as sizable as his wife was tiny. If size mattered, they were mismatched. Yet in every other way, they seemed attentive to one another and were holding hands as they sat on the edge of the bench, looking expectantly at the old timer.

"Uh, yeah, I met these folks before," he answered, and tipped his hat to the woman.

"Well, I've been talkin' a little to Nathan and Naomi 'bout those young'uns that Tate told us about. You saw 'em and you talked to Tate 'bout 'em, what can you tell these folks?"

Charley squirmed a little, accepted a cup of coffee from Morgan and found a seat on an upturned nail-keg. He sipped while he thought and looked to the young couple and said, "Wal, I only saw 'em fer a real short while, I was in a hurry to get back an' warn the wagons 'bout the Crow war party. But, they looked like fine youngsters. Tate said they was 'bout fifteen and they was the only ones whut survived the attack on their train."

"Oh, my, those poor dears," said Naomi, putting her hand to her mouth, and looking to her husband.

"Are they brother an' sister?" asked Nathan.

"Uh, no, I don' think so. When Tate was talkin' 'bout findin' 'em, he said the boy, I think his name is Ira, had shot a Injun just 'bout the time the Injun was 'bout to strike the girl. Then he snuck her back in the trees an' stayed hid til Tate come on 'em."

"Well, that speaks well o' the boy. He stepped up an' did

what he had to an' helped the girl," surmised Nathan, nodding his head and looking to his woman.

She nodded in agreement, and looked to Charley again, "Do they want to go with us?"

"Uh, ma'am, I cain't rightly say, but they ain't used to the woods, an' these mountains shore ain't no place fer 'em. I s'pose you'd need to ask them that question."

Morgan spoke up and asked, "Could you take the Johnston's to Tate's cabin to meet these young folks?"

"Sure, sure. From here it'd take, oh, maybe less'n half a day to get there. That'd give ya' time to meet 'em, talk to 'em and decide. Then we could be back hyar 'bout noon tomorrow."

Nathan looked to Morgan and asked, "Can we spare that much time?"

"Sure. I wasn't plannin' on leavin' til day after tomorrow anyway!"

Nathan looked to Charley, "We'll be ready in two shakes of a lamb's tail!"

Charley stood, cup in hand and answered, "Wal, I ain't seen no lambs hereabouts, but I'll be back hyar in a jiffy."

TATE AND WHISKERS were walking around the cabin when they heard the clatter of more hooves on the trail. Tate reached for his ever-present Dragoon and paused at the corner of the cabin, waiting to see who was approaching. Whiskers was at his side and asked, "Ain't that the ol' man from the wagons?"

Tate squinted and recognized Charley, grinning from under his gray and brown whiskers, gray from age and brown from tobacco, and Charley waved his hand overhead and hollered, "Howdy!" Behind him rode two others, a man and a woman, neither familiar to Tate, but he relaxed and walked toward the visitors.

"Well, howdy Charley! Didn't 'spect to see you again. Step on down, you know you're welcome."

Charley reined up and swung his leg over the rump of his horse, acting like his bones were creaking from lack of grease, and spotted the coffee cup in Tate's hand and asked, "Got any more o' that thar Arbuckles?"

"Oh, I think we can find some," he motioned the old timer to tether their horses at the rail below the porch and turned to introduce himself to the visitors. Extending his hand to the big man, he said, "Howdy, I'm Tate Saint, and this tame grizzly is Whiskers."

"I remember you Mr. Saint, we're from the wagon train," he turned to help his wife down and Tate noted she had a pair of man's britches on under her long dress, so she could ride astraddle of the horse. He knew that was not the common practice among white women, but the Indian women often wore leggings under their long tunics or dresses, a practice Maggie had adopted from her first time in the mountains with Tate.

"I'm Nathan Johnston, and this is my wife, Naomi."

Tate tipped his hat, as did Whiskers, "Pleased to meet you ma'am. How 'bout you folks havin' a seat on the porch there, an' I'll fetch you some coffee. I'd have you inside, but my wife's ailin' an' she's bein' tended to by Whiskers' wife."

"Sorry to hear that, Tate. Was it Injuns?" asked Charley.

"Yup, but with a lot o' care and more prayer, I'm hopin' she'll be alright."

"Wal, 'fore you go in fer that coffee, let me explain

sumpin. After you spoke to Cap'n Morgan 'bout them young'uns from the wagons, wal, these folks'd like to meet 'em and see if they might, y'know, make a family."

Tate looked from Charley to the Johnston's and back to Charley, chuckled and said, "We were just talkin' 'bout that this mornin'. That's the first time I've been around here to talk 'bout it an' it's good you folk are here." He thought a moment then suggested, "How 'bout I tell 'em bout you bein' here and then maybe you'ns could all take a walk down toward the lake yonder an' spend some time together. You know, to get to know one another and get your questions answered."

Nathan and Naomi looked at one another, smiling and nodding their heads enthusiastically. Tate pushed through the door and entered to whispers and giggles as the four youngsters were busy tidying up the cabin. The clean-up from the morning meal was done and they were getting ready to go outside, but when the visitors arrived, they stayed inside and were trying to guess who was there. When Tate stepped in, they stopped talking and looked to him, waiting for what he was about to say, expecting answers to their guesses.

He pulled a chair away from the table and addressing the two older youngsters, "Remember what we were talkin' 'bout at breakfast?"

Both Ira and Vicky slowly nodded their heads, and Ira answered, "Uh, yeah, if you mean about what we wanted to do, we remember."

"Well, I told you there were some folks that might like to fill in for your ma and pa, well, they're outside."

Ira and Vicky looked at Tate, at one another, and back

to Tate. Vicky asked, "They want to take us now?" fear showing in her voice.

"No, no. They just want to get to know you. You're not going anywhere, unless you want to, but you need to get to know them before you make any decision. I don't know anything about them, but I do know Charley and the wagon master, and they wouldn't recommend them if they weren't fine folks. So, I suggested you all go for a walk down toward the lake, talk a spell, and get all your questions answered and get to know one another. Would that be alright?"

They looked to one another again and slowly nodded their heads back to Tate. Vicky asked again, "But what if we don't like them or don't want to go with them?"

"Then you'll stay right here until you decide what you want to do."

Reassured, the two young friends stood and started for the door. Tate stopped them and asked, "But could you first pour us some coffee, if there's enough, that is?"

CHAPTER THIRTY-ONE
CHANGES

TATE LEFT WHISKERS AND CHARLEY TO THEIR reminiscences of the old days and went to check on Maggie and Red Hawk. When he entered the room, Maggie was awake and showing her discomfort. Red Hawk had replaced many of the poultices and added more on other wounds, and looked up to Tate, "Good, you help, need wrap her here," motioning to the midriff of Maggie and the area of her broken ribs. "Need tight wrap, help her breathe and heal." She stood up beside the bed and motioned Tate to the other side. She picked up a bundle of buckskin strips, each about six inches wide and some as long as six feet. Tate thought those had to have been cut the full length of a bigbuck skin to be that long in one piece. She lay them flat alongside Maggie on the bed and began to explain to Tate, "You lift here and here," motioning to the shoulders and her rump. "I will put these under legs and head, you must not move. I will wrap with longest bands, then you put down."

Tate nodded his head in understanding but as he

considered what he must do, he realized it would be difficult to hold her entire weight still while Red Hawk wrapped the buckskin around her middle. He watched while she readied the pillows and rolled up blankets that would support her head and legs, positioned the straps for easy reach, and she looked to Tate and nodded. All the while, Maggie watched, and her eyes showed wide and white, fearful of the pain she knew was coming. Her breath was ragged, and her pain was evident, but the ribs had to be stabilized to prevent any further damage to her insides. They couldn't wrap her with Maggie sitting up, as it would put too much pressure on her ribs as she leaned forward. Tate knew the dangers of broken ribs and had known of others that had their insides ripped apart by the jagged ends, and they eventually died a painful death. He was afraid for Maggie and was determined to do whatever was necessary to prevent her having any pain, if possible.

He breathed deep, put one stabilizing knee on the edge of the bed and looked to Red Hawk. She did a quick check that all was ready, looked to Tate and slowly nodded. He reached out with his left arm to slowly slip it under her shoulders, careful not to move her. Then the right arm under her thighs, but Red Hawk spoke, "No, no! Under here," pointing to her lower back at her tailbone, "must keep back straight!" she demanded. Tate nodded and moved his arm up, realizing if he picked her up too far below the waist, that would cause her to tighten up her stomach muscles and her midriff and possibly move her ribs. Red Hawk looked at the placement of his arms, and then to Tate, "Now, slow."

Tate took another deep breath, and slowly lifted

Maggie off the bed, with her using her good right arm to help stabilize herself. Red Hawk quickly moved the pillows beneath her head, and the rolled-up blankets beneath her legs. Just that much relieved some of the weight, but Tate held her, unmoving, as Red Hawk worked rapidly to begin her binding. Tate easily held her for the first few moments, but the weight and the tension began to tell. He felt his biceps beginning to tighten, cramp, and protest. His forearms were tight and shooting pain began climbing up his arms. His forehead showed drops of sweat and he forced a smile as he looked into the eyes of his beloved redhead.

Red Hawk had wrapped the two long strips of buckskin around her middle careful to make them tight and smooth and began tying them off. Within seconds, she nodded and removed the pillows, so Tate could lower Maggie to the bed. He grimaced as the cramped muscles rebelled, but he gritted his teeth, and carefully lay her down and slid his arms from beneath her. Maggie too was grimacing but forced a smile as Tate stood beside her. She gently lay her hands on the bindings, slowly took a deep breath, and sighed and said, "Yes, that's better."

Tate looked to Red Hawk and said, "Is there anything else I can do?"

Red Hawk looked to Maggie, felt her brow, and said to Tate, "She needs cold, she is too hot, must have cold."

"You mean like snow or ice?" asked Tate, bewildered, not understanding what was happening.

"Bad cuts, leg and arm, more." She touched her own forehead and said, "Hot, must be cool. I give tea to help but need more."

"The water in the little creek yonder is pretty cold, would that help?"

"Yes, but ice or snow better," she responded, looking to Maggie who was showing drops of sweat on her forehead and neck. She had flipped all covers aside, and showed she was hot.

Tate had seen the signs before of someone burning up with fever and knew that was usually an infection, and infection at this stage could be deadly. He thought for a moment, then remembered, "I know where there's an ice cave, it'll take me awhile to get there and back, but I'll be back by dark!" He bent down to give Maggie a light kiss and whispered, "You hang on sweetheart, I'll be back soon." She smiled and squeezed his hand and he hurried from the room.

He grabbed a spare blanket, picked up his Sharps and possibles bag, and started from the cabin.

Whiskers and Charley turned as Tate erupted through the door and Whiskers asked, "What's goin' on? Maggie alright?" he questioned as he stood to look to his friend.

"She needs some ice, she's burning up with fever, an' I'm goin' to an ice cave I know to fetch her some."

"Wal, I'll just go with ya' if that's alright?" asked the big man.

Charley looked at the two and said, "You go on, I reckon I better stay here on account o' them others," referring to the Johnston's and the youngsters.

Tate nodded and said to Whiskers, "Well, c'mon, time's a wastin'!"

IT WAS LESS than an hour later when the riders broke from

the thick cluster of skinny fir and came out next to a huge upthrust of limestone. Whiskers looked about and saw other similar stone formations, but this was the largest. He lifted his eyes and the jagged flat surface appeared as a wall that stood over a hundred feet high and twice as wide and seemed to be supported by nothing, although the back side shouldered off at a steep angle and the clinging dirt held tufts of grasses and cacti. The front face was in the shadow, but the pale gray stone was imposing and hung at a slight angle over them as it stretched heavenward. Tate started toward a narrow cleft with the straps of the big rawhide parfleche over his shoulder and looked back to see if Whiskers was coming.

The big man stepped down from his mount, tethered him beside the Grulla, and started after Tate as he ducked into the cleft. Tate paused at the edge of the light, pulled a candle from his coat pocket and a small metal box from which he brought out a small stick. Whiskers frowned and watched his friend and suddenly jumped back when a small flame flared up and Tate lit the candle. Whiskers asked, "What'd you just do?"

Tate chuckled and replied, "Oh, that's one o' them *loco focos*. A new thing fer startin' fires. Don't use 'em much, but they sure come in handy in places like this. Here, here's another candle," handing it to Whiskers and using his own to light it.

Whiskers followed close behind Tate, not liking the dark cave or any place that seemed too confining, but he kept pace with his friend. The passage way seemed to be going down deeper, a slope of ground, littered with small shards of rock, and with the walls smooth and appearing wet and wrinkled.

Tate slowed, and stopped before a wall that reflected the light and Whiskers stepped closer, both men feeling the cold. The deep blue of the barrier appeared to be a frozen waterfall, and Tate took his big Bowie and began chopping at it, breaking off several sizable chunks. Whiskers copied his friend and they soon had enough to fill the parfleche.

Tate pulled the blanket from the parfleche, folded it and put the end back into the container, and began placing the chunks of blue ice in the parfleche.

Whiskers was handing the chunks to Tate and said, "It shore is nice an' cold in hyar. This ice is sumpin'. Is it like this all year?"

"I think so. Ever time I've been in here, it seems to slowly get bigger, the ice, I mean. But only been here a couple times before. No need."

The parfleche was soon full and Tate folded the blanket over the top of the ice before closing the flap. Within moments, the two men and their special cargo were on their way back to the cabin. As expected, the sun was just settling down to rest on the western horizon when they rode into the clearing by the cabin. Tate stepped down and went up the porch steps, nodded to Charley and walked in to give the ice to Red Hawk. When she opened the parfleche, she looked up to Tate with surprise, but happy eyes told him she was pleased. She soon had a thin cloth with small chunks of ice on Maggie's forehead and another on both sides of her neck. Maggie's eyes were closed, but fluttered open as she felt the cold, and looked to Red Hawk, and slowly nodded her head in appreciation. Her eyes closed, and she lay quietly, breathing easier than before, but her face had a slightly gray pallor and Tate was worried. He asked Red Hawk again, "Anything else I can do?"

"It is up to the Great Spirit," said Red Hawk as she seated herself beside the bed and gently took Maggie's hand in hers. Tate sighed, and turned away to go outside. He knew the others, especially the children, were concerned and wanted to know how Maggie was doing and he had to talk to them.

Whiskers had put up the horses and was climbing the steps to the porch when Tate came from the cabin. The upturned faces of Charley, Whiskers, Sean, and Sadie asked the unspoken question and Tate sat down to explain everything. "Whenever someone has these kinds of injuries and so many of 'em, there's always the danger of infection. Not just from the cuts an' such, but also from the broken bones like the ribs an all. Whenever there's infection, there's usually a temperature, and they start sweatin' and getting' real hot. My ma used to tell me that's the body fightin' and doin' it's best to get rid of the infection. That's why we got the ice, to help her get rid of the infection and the fever. It's gonna take a while, but our Maggie's a fighter and if we do what we can and pray for her, then I'm thinkin' she'll be alright."

Tate sat with his elbows on his knees, hands clasped together, and looked from one to another of those before him. Sadie rose from her seat on the top step and went to her pa and put her hand on his shoulder and said, "Momma's gonna get better, I know it, Pa. Don't worry."

Tate had to grin at the simple faith of his child and reached out to give her a big bear hug. Sean was a little jealous and stepped to the other side of his pa and waited for his hug, and he wasn't disappointed. Tate had just sat back, an arm around each child standing beside him, when he looked up to see the Johnston's, Ira, and Vicky returning from their walk. Everyone was smiling, and it appeared they had come to a decision about the future of the two youngsters, who walked hand in hand and smiling at one another. Tate turned to Charley and spoke softly, "Looks like they're all happy. You might have a couple more to take back to the wagons."

"Hehehehe, I kinda figgered that might happen, by gum, yessir I did," responded Charley, showing his own whisker parting grin.

Tate stood and greeted the returnees, "Wal, looks like you all had a good walk." Then looking to the Johnston's, "How'd you like our little corner of the world?"

Nathan looked up with a wide grin, "It's sure beautiful country, but a mite wild to suit me."

Tate grinned and thought by that response, they all would be headed to Oregon and a settlement with lots of other people around and very few wild animals and Indians.

THE TWO YOUNGSTERS WERE MORE EXCITED THAN A BOY with his hand stuck in a cookie jar. They talked over one another as they sought to tell Tate about all they had learned and discussed with the Johnston's. The two had scampered up the stairs to the porch and stood in front of Tate with Vicky starting, "Oh, Tate, Mrs. Johnston is a dressmaker and she said she could teach me how to make my own dresses, and children's clothes, and . . . and . . . and . . . anything else I wanted!"

"Yeah and remember how I said I wanted a trade where I could work with my hands?" asked Ira, continuing without waiting for an answer, "Mr. Johnston is a blacksmith and a wheelwright, and he said he'd be proud to teach me everything I would need to know to be one too!"

Nathan and Naomi stood at the bottom of the stairs smiling and he pulled her close as they listened to the excited youngsters share everything they discussed. Their eyes glowed with their own enthusiasm about having the two young people join them in their home and becoming a part of their family.

"And," started Vicky, pausing and a little embarrassed, "they said if Ira and I wanted to be together, you know, married an' all, they would be happy for us and do everything they could to help us get a home and everything." She looked to Ira, who smiled and dropped his head.

"Well, that all sounds mighty fine, but I hope you two won't be gettin' hitched right away, are ya'?" asked Tate, grinning.

Ira lifted his wide eyes to look at Tate, "Oh no! No! We won't be doin' that for a long time! I've got to learn the trade an...a ...well, you know," he stammered, trying to explain what he didn't understand.

Tate chuckled, "Ah, I was just funnin' you! But I take it this means you've decided to go with these fine folks?"

"Uh, mostly, but they said they won't be leaving til in the morning, and that we should think and pray about it tonight, and if we still feel the same way tomorrow, then they want us to come with them. Is that alright?" asked Vicky, concerned.

"Of course, that's alright. And maybe by morning, Maggie'll be feelin' better and can tell you goodbye."

A look of dread came across Vicky's face as she whispered, "She's alright, isn't she? Oh, I hope so, she means so much."

Tate dropped his eyes, and his facial expression subdued, "She's struggling with a fever now, but Red Hawk's taking good care of her. I'm sure she'll be fine." He wasn't as confident as he tried to sound. "But for right now, we need to be startin' our supper," he rose from the chair and started for the door, but Vicky stopped him with her hand on his chest.

"I told you before, let me take care of that, you tend to, well, whatever you need to tend to!" and turned to the door and said, "C'mon, Ira, you can help get the fire goin'," and motioned for him to join her.

Naomi started up the stairs with, "Don't forget me! If there's going to be any cooking done, I want to help!" Vicky smiled at her and motioned for her to join them as they went through the door to begin their magic at the stove and fireplace.

It was a pleasant supper and as Nathan pushed back from the table and patted his sizable middle, "Wal, with two great cooks, I'm liable to end up big as a house!" he declared and laughed, making his newly stuffed stomach bounce, prompting the others to join in the levity.

Charley looked at the others, cleared his throat and said, "Wal, when ever'body was busy with their walks and fetchin', I kinda figgered us men might need a place to throw our bedrolls, so I put together a bit of a lean-to o'er yonder by the crick. What with so many wimmen folks, there ain't room in this hyar cabin. Sound right to you Tate?"

"That's kinda what I figgered too, Charley. But, I didn't reckon on no lean-to, you thinkin' it might storm on us?"

"Muh bones say so, an' they ain't wrong too often!"

Tate looked to Ira, "How 'bout you fetchin' a couple bedrolls from the tack shed and bring along a couple o' them saddle blankets as well." He turned to the others, "You fellas can pitch your camp, and I'll be along after a bit. I need to see to Maggie first." He rose from his chair and went to the bedroom while the others stood and started on their designated duties.

Red Hawk rose from the chair beside the bed and walked to the door, looked back at Tate and turned to go to the table and fix herself a plate of supper. Tate sat beside his wife, looked at her face, and she seemed to be breathing easier. He touched her brow, felt the fever but believed it to be less than before and whispered, "Maggie, I love you, I have always loved you and I need you, the kids need you, so keep fighting. You can beat this, I know you can!" Her eyes fluttered but did not open, a soft groan escaped from her lips and she moved her head slowly side to side. Her forehead wrinkled, and she appeared to be scowling, but then relaxed and lay still, once again breathing easy. Tate picked up her hand and looked at the long slender fingers and the smooth skin, tanned with the many days in the warm sun of the mountains, and he looked at her pale face. The pallor accenting the freckles that marched across the bridge of her nose and the red hair that tumbled to the sides, *She is beautiful* thought the man, letting a slow smile cover his face.

He whispered again, "Maggie, I love you more than life itself! Don't ever forget you are loved and will always be loved," he took a deep breath and added, "So please, Babe, please come back to me!"

The door opened, and Red Hawk moved to the bedside, a plate in her hands, and looked down to Maggie. Tate looked at the woman and softly spoke, "Red Hawk, thank you for all you've done and are doing. You're a fine friend."

She looked at the man, tried to retain her somber expression but her eyes danced as she spoke, "She is my friend and sister. You go now, go spend time with the Great Spirit, I stay."

Tate nodded and rose from the chair, looked again at Maggie, bent to kiss her on the forehead, and left the room. Naomi and Vicky were busy at the counter, Sadie was helping by clearing the table under their watchful eyes, and the camaraderie was evident as Tate walked by them. As he left the cabin, he looked to the small campfire to the side of the clearing and saw the men readying their bedrolls and he waved as he walked, "I'll be back in a little bit. Gonna spend some time down yonder, prayin'. Don't wait up fer me!" They waved back, and Tate walked to his customary prayer bench that sat in the small clearing just below the shoulder of the cabin site. It was situated to catch the first light of the morning as the sun topped the mountains in the east and now the colors of the sunset wrapped around him, casting a long shadow before him. And Tate was glad for the solitude, it had been a busy and noisy day.

As HE SAT for a long while on the bench, he leaned back and lay his Bible on the seat beside him. He looked to the sky, now black but covered so thickly with bright stars he felt he could reach up and pluck them from the darkness. Off his right shoulder, the half-moon hung as if it were the captain of the night ship that would sail the milky way. "Ahoy matey!" came the cry from his imagination, and he smiled at the memory of other dark nights he

enjoyed lying on his back and staring at the constella-
tions, trying to remember those told him by his school
teacher father. His youth had been a pleasant time,
running through the nearby woods, hunting with his
Osage friend, Red Calf, and learning about the wilderness
and the history of the world from his father. But it was his
mother who guided him on his spiritual path, and he was
thankful to both parents. They had given him a carefree
childhood, and even though he lost them before he
reached manhood, they seemed to walk with him every
day and their teachings made him a man.

His thoughts turned to Maggie and he began to pray
and as he whispered the words, scripture after scripture
came to his mind, as if God Himself was reminding him
of the power of prayer. *The effectual, fervent prayer of a
righteous man availeth much. Pray without ceasing. Ask and it
shall be given you, seek and ye shall find, knock and it shall be
opened unto you. And the prayer of faith shall save the sick, and
the Lord shall raise him up. Pray for one another that ye may
be healed.* He dropped his face to his hands and let the
tears flow through his fingers and he prayed.

He leaned back and looked to the stars again, realizing
he was empty of words to say, but was reminded of the
verse, *Likewise the Spirit also helpeth our infirmities: for we
know not what we should pray for as we ought: but the Spirit
itself maketh intercession for us with groanings that cannot be
uttered.* Romans 8:26. His mother told him that when he
was burdened in his spirit or heart and didn't know what
to say to the Lord, to just remember that the Holy Spirit
knows your heart and would take those burdens to the
throne of God on your behalf, speaking what you cannot
find the words to say. Tate relaxed and thought of how

blessed he was with a wonderful wife, who he considered was a gift from God, and two wonderful children that had shown themselves time and again to be special blessings. And he prayed.

Inside at the table, the ladies had finished their clean-up and gathered around. Red Hawk came from the bedroom with her plate and sat it on the counter and turned to the others as Naomi said, "Red Hawk, we are going to pray for Maggie. Would you like to join us?" Red Hawk looked at the women, nodded, and took a seat at the table. Naomi reached out to join hands with Vicky and Red Hawk as those women took the hands of Sadie. Naomi began, "Our Father in heaven, . . ." and continued as she made imprecation for the mutual friend, but a woman she had not even met.

AT THE CAMPFIRE, Nathan looked at the boys, Ira and Sean, then to the men and said, "Fellas, I'm thinkin' we oughta be prayin' for that special lady lyin' in yonder. Now, I ain't never met her, but she's got a mighty fine family and friends, so, what say we pray for her?"

Whiskers and Charley squirmed a little as they looked to the big blacksmith, and then to the boys, and Whiskers said, "I ain't never been one fer prayin', don't really know how. But if'n you wanna be doin' it, then that'll be fine, don'tcha reckon, Charley?"

The old timer looked at the two big men, and the two young'uns and nodded his head as he doffed his hat and said, "Go 'head on!"

Nathan dropped his head, chin to his chest, and began praying, "Lord, we're comin' to you with a special need.

There's a fine woman in the cabin yonder that's needin' your healin', so Lord, we're askin' . . . " and he continued lifting their prayer to the God of heaven. When he finished, he said "Amen" and was echoed by the others around the fire.

CHAPTER THIRTY-THREE
PARTING

IT WAS THE DIM LIGHT OF EARLY MORNING WHEN THE HINT of the sun barely silhouetted the eastern mountains. Tate stared at the shadowy horizon as he crossed his legs and breathed deep of the cool morning air. He bent down, resting his elbows on his knees and put his chin in his hands as he stared and thought about the years he and Maggie had enjoyed together. The many times they explored the mountains as they hunted for their winter's meat supply, the happy times of chasing toddlers in the tall grasses and watching them play with Lobo and the bear cub Buster. They were a happy family and he thanked the Lord for every day, every moment, they were together. His heart groaned within him at the thought that these days could end. He breathed deep and leaned back, and began reciting the Lord's prayer, learned so many years ago at his mother's knee. He finished with another "Amen," whispered aloud.

The first lances of pale yellow and pink stretched above the horizon, announcing the arrival of another day and Tate smiled at the wonder of God's creation. A low growl came from behind him and he started to turn, but the familiar voice of Whiskers asked, "Couldja use some comp'ny?"

"Sure, sure, have a seat," answered Tate, picking up his Bible and scooting to the end of the bench, making room for the big man.

"You been out here all night?" asked the man mountain as he seated himself.

Tate chuckled and answered, "Guess I have, didn't mean to, but . . . " and let the thought trail off as he lifted his eyes to the wide panorama of pink and pale yellow that God painted across the eastern sky.

"I understand, don' know whut I'd be doin' if'n it was Red Hawk down like that." He paused a moment and mumbled, "We prayed fer Maggie last night."

Tate turned to look at the big man, forehead wrinkled in wonder and surprise, "You did?"

"Wal, not me in particular, but that other feller, the blacksmith, he prayed an' we listened. Don't that count?"

Tate chuckled and answered, "Of course," and he turned to look back to the east.

Whiskers squirmed a little, shuffled his feet and leaned forward, elbows on his knees, and spoke over his shoulder, "Uh, there's sumpin' I been wonderin' 'bout. I've known 'boutchu since that first rendezvous, an' you're a man of the mountains and you're known to be a man ta' ride the river with, and yet you know yore way 'round that book." He pointed to the Bible on Tate's lap. "An' there seems to be somethin' a bit different 'boutchu, I mean you read that thar book, an' you pray and such, but it's more'n that. Like when you took off after that Crow whut took yore woman, you did like any man of the mountains would do, and from what you said you done him in proper. But then I see you by your woman's bed, an' out here a prayin', an' I ain't never seen nobody do that. I mean, some o' them preacher types tell ya' it ain't right to kill them Injuns, an' ya oughta be some mealy-mouthed milquetoast sissy britches. Cuz o' that, I ain't never wanted nuthin' to do with religion. But you ain't like that." He shook his head and dropped his chin to his chest in consternation, wanting a believable answer.

Tate looked at the big man, and he leaned forward, assuming the same position beside his friend, elbows on knees and hands clasped as they watched the sunrise together. He took a deep breath and began, "Whiskers, I was fortunate that I had a godly mother who taught me about things of the Bible when I was a youngster. And I was fortunate to have a father that helped me apply those truths to my life as a man. My faith has nothing to do with other people, or how others try to show their religion like some of those you spoke about, but it is that personal friendship with the Lord of the Bible. When you get that right, then the rest of life begins to fall into place. When I accepted Christ as my savior, I was an ornery youngster that didn't want anything to do with school or church or anything that came with civilization. I'd rather go runnin' through the woods, huntin' with my friend, anything but what my Ma wanted. But when she explained that nothing was more important than that bond with Christ, I began to listen to what she and the Bible had to say.

"Whiskers, the first thing God wants for us is for each of us to know Him as personal savior. That's what it takes to make sure of Heaven. And when we know that Heaven is our home, we won't be so fearful of dying, and without that fear, that when life begins to make sense. We learn how to relate to our fellow man, creation, our lives together, everything."

"But," interrupted Whiskers, "If you learn how to get along, how can you go out an' kill an Injun like that Crow?"

"Well, that's something that takes a while to understand, but simply, it's like this. God hates evil, even more than we do, and that Crow leader was evil and everything he was doing was evil. I don't argue with those that think they need to defend their land, their families, their way of life, because that's what I was doing when I went after him. But all he wanted to do was murder and steal, and he wasn't particular who it was or why they were in his way, he was evil and that showed when he took Maggie. So, I was just defending my family against evil. That doesn't mean the way it's done is best of that I won't make mistakes and make some bad choices, but, He's always there to help us do right and forgive us when we ask."

"So, God doesn't think that's bad?" asked the big man.

"No, we are supposed to protect and provide for our families. It doesn't matter if it's a grizzly bear, a charging bull elk, or a crazed Indian, we must protect them."

"An' you're sayin' that if I had that same kinda friendship with God, I'd do better understandin' those things?"

Tate thought for a moment and said, "Remember when you first came to the mountains and you joined up with other trappers?"

"Yeah, I had to, cuz I didn't know nuthin'."

"Same thing with God. It's like 'joining up' with God when you accept His gift of eternal life and then you spend time with Him in prayer and the Bible and you learn more about what the life He wants for you is all about."

"So, how do I do this 'joinin' up'?"

"Simple, there's a few things it helps to understand. One, the Bible says we're all sinners, You know that don't you, that you're a sinner?"

"Boy howdy! I reckon that's right."

"And because we're sinners, the penalty for that sin is death and hell forever. That's told about in Romans 6:23. But God doesn't want that for us, He wants us to have eternal life and He bought that with Christ dying for us, Romans 5:8, 6:23. And it's a gift that He offers to us freely and all we have to do is ask Him for that gift, *Romans 10:9-13.* So, if you want to get started, all we need to do is go to the Lord in prayer and ask Him for forgiveness and accept His gift of eternal life, which is life forever in Heaven."

Tate paused and looked to Whiskers and the man sat back to look to Tate and asked, "Can we do that? I mean, that forgiveness and Heaven stuff?"

"Sure, tell ya what. I'll start prayin' and you can listen in and I'll lead you when you need to pray, alright?"

"Ummhumm," he answered and bowed his head.

Tate began by thanking the Lord for His work in their lives and led Whiskers to ask God for forgiveness and to receive that free gift of eternal life and to help him learn how to live as God would have him live.

When they finished, Whiskers lifted his head, smiling and reached over to give Tate a big bear hug that Tate thought was squeezing the life out of him, then leaned back and said, "Thanks, I shore needed that."

As Tate and Whiskers walked back toward the porch, they were greeted by Charley, holding his shirttail up, showing his hairy belly, and cackling like a mother hen. Tate asked, "What's with you, old timer?"

"Hehehehe, looky here what I got!" and he pulled the shirttail out to reveal a half dozen duck eggs. "Put some thin strips o' deer steak with them an' you'll have a mighty fine breakfast, yessiree!"

"Well, your bones weren't right about that storm, but we'll be glad for what your belly pouch has for us. Let's see if any o' them women are awake in there," answered Tate, nodding toward the cabin. "They'd probably be pleased to add that to the mornin' fare."

And pleased they were. Everyone was up early, anticipating the journey back to the wagons and the start of their new life and knew they would travel better on a full stomach. The women had already mixed up a good batch of cornbread muffins and had them cooking. The thin slices of deer meat were about ready for the frying pan and when they saw the eggs their eyes lit up with surprise and Vicky said, "Well, there's not enough for one a piece, but if we scramble 'em up with the meat, everybody'll get plenty!"

It was an enjoyable breakfast, although some were excited about leaving and others sad to see them go, and they all dallied around the table, not wanting to set this change in motion. But Charley stood, "Wal, folks. We better git ta goin', don' want them wagons leavin' without us!"

Naomi looked to Charley, fearful, and asked, "They wouldn't leave, would they?"

Charley chuckled and answered, "Prob'ly not, but don'

wanna take a chance. It's a mighty long way to Oregon an' we gotta make time fore the snow flies!"

Tate had given the two pack horses to the youngsters, but he didn't have a saddle to spare so he made a pad with a couple of blankets and they were pleased with the gifts. Maggie was only semi-conscious, still fighting the fever, and was unable to say goodbye, but Vicky and Ira asked Tate to relay their thanks and love. The sun stood less than a hand above the eastern horizon when the group rode from the clearing and disappeared into the trees as they took the trail back to South Pass.

Tate and Whiskers returned to the porch and Sean and Sadie played in the clearing with Lobo. Whiskers said, "Those were fine folks, and them younguns are mighty lucky."

"Yes, they are and I'm happy for Ira and Vicky. Just a week ago, they had no idea what they were going to do with their lives, and now they've got a great future. But, even though they were only here a few days, I'm gonna miss 'em."

"Ummmhummmm," mumbled Whiskers as he listened to the dwindling sounds of hooves on the trail. "Now, what'chu gonna do 'bout pack horses?"

"I just happen to know somebody that has more horses than he needs," grinned Tate.

IT WAS A LITTLE AFTER NOON THE NEXT DAY WHEN Maggie's temperature broke and everyone seemed to breathe a sigh of relief. Smiles were seen every now and then and the air whispered a little clearer, and the sky a little bluer. But Red Hawk refused to leave Maggie's side, so the men were tasked with the cooking duties, which they took to more familiar surroundings and did outside over the campfire at the edge of the clearing.

But even with the men busy at the fire, Tate found time to be at Maggie's side and after a couple days, his presence began to be a bother to Red Hawk. She suggested to Whiskers they take the trip to get the replacement horses for Tate.

Tate asked, "But, who's gonna mind the kids and do the cooking?"

Maggie giggled and said, "I'm sure Red Hawk knows her way around a campfire, and the little ones will be a big help. Besides, you're not going to be gone more'n a couple days."

"Alright, if you're sure?" he asked as he bent to give her a kiss.

"I'm sure, now go on and get goin' so you can get back!" she instructed.

He chuckled and left the bedroom. Both men were happy to be hitting the trail again and Tate was pleased they were taking Sean with them. They didn't waste any time getting the horses rigged and their gear together. Tate mounted up and reined Shady around and went to the bedroom window, leaned down to look in and said, "We'll be back probably tomorrow evenin'. So, you women try to behave while we're gone!" he chuckled then saw Sadie sitting on the edge of the bed and added, "An' Sadie, you take care of your ma now, understand?"

"Sure, Pa. I will," answered the enthusiastic Sadie.

Tate reined around and the three were soon on the trail to the Arapaho village and the small herd of horses that Whiskers was so proud of and would hopefully provide good replacement mounts for Tate and family. Sean still brooded a little about losing his Dusty, but he was anxious to find another. He looked to Whiskers and asked, "You got any steeldust horses?"

Whiskers thought a moment and said, "Ya' know, I don't. But there's several nice horses to choose from, an' I'm sure you'll find yourself a nice 'un."

"I hope so, cuz Dusty was a mighty fine horse. That Crow musta known a lot 'bout horses cuz he sure picked the best one to steal!" grumbled the boy.

The men looked to one another, chuckled and gigged their horses to a trot to make a little better time. Although as the crow flies, the village of the Arapaho was no more than ten or eleven miles away, but following the trail over the challenging terrain, it took almost a half day to make the journey. It was early afternoon when they rode into the village and went to the lodge of Red Pipe. He was pleased to see the men and they took a while to sit and visit, with Sean antsy and wandering about until a youngster about his age approached and with hand signs and a few words, took Sean away to play a hoop game with the others.

Before Red Pipe would let the men go look at the horses, he made them agree to come back to his lodge to have a meal together and they quickly agreed. Tate and Whiskers started toward the horse herd and waved to Sean to join them as they walked. Whiskers explained, "I got some youngsters that watch o'er muh horses, but they watch some o' the others too, so I took to markin' mine to keep 'em straight. Most Injuns know which is theirs just by the look of 'em, but I trade so often, I started markin' 'em. All o' mine have a strip o' ribbon braided into their manes, Red Hawk did that fer me, an' you can tell 'em that way. But, if you see 'nother horse that ain't mine, we might be able to finagle a trade fer ya'. Mebbe, but cain't say fer sure."

As they walked up to the herd, they saw a rock formation to the side and climbed atop to get a better look. Sean was the first to spot one of interest and spoke up, "Look at that one Pa, the one with the white rump and spots on it. There," he pointed to the edge of the herd, "That one. See him?" He had picked out a fine appaloosa that showed spirit with his uplifted head and high stepping walk. The horse pushed the others aside as he made his way through the herd, retreating from the visitors, but moving to the edge of the horse herd, then stopped to look back at those on the rocks. He stood, ears forward, staring and moving all the time, but not nervous, just curious.

Whiskers spoke up and said, "I traded that'n from some Nez Perce when I took a trip up north o' here. Got a couple of 'em, fine horses and they got spirit. That'n you're lookin' at is a stallion, an' the other, over yonder, see?" He pointed toward the back of the herd to another horse with similar markings but covering more than just the rump. "That's a mare, an' I'm thinkin' they'd make a good pair fer breedin', if'n that's what's yore thinkin'." He looked to Tate to see if he was interested. But Tate was looking at the herd and showed no particular interest.

Tate pointed out a red dun and asked, "That big dun yonder, he your'n?"

"Yeah, he is. He's gelded an' broke gentle. I won him in a game o' bones from an old man here in the village. I'm thinkin' he's 'bout ten or so. There's another'n that'd make a good pack-horse, that black'n there at the back."

Tate looked at the one he pointed out, then scanned the rest of the herd and leaned back and said, "Tell ya what, I'll keep that dapple-gray I borrowed from you, and them two appaloosa and the red dun. I'll trade you the Hawken I took off that Crow, and I'll give you, oh, twenty dollars gold coin. How's that?"

"I dunno, that gray's a fine animal an' so's them two appaloosa. Make it forty dollars gold coin an' the Hawken, an' we got a deal!"

Sean was looking from his pa to Whiskers, and back again, listening to their bickering and when Whiskers countered, he looked to his pa with his most sorrowful and hopeful look and Tate glanced at him and grinned.

"Looks like the boy wants that appy pretty bad, so,

alright. We got us a deal." The men shook hands and started off the rocks. Whiskers went to the young men watching the horses and explained what he would need, come morning, and they nodded in understanding and Tate and Whiskers returned to the camp and Red Pipe's lodge.

SEAN HAD RIDDEN Maggie's buckskin to the village and would ride her back, but he was also tasked with leading the appaloosa stallion he had chosen as his own. With a braided halter and lead rope, the animal was docile and easily led. Whiskers led the dun and Tate led the appaloosa mare. It was an uneventful return to the cabin and as they neared, the horses were curious and turned about looking at the new surroundings. But the big surprise was to see Maggie sitting on the porch with Red Hawk by her side and smiling as they rode into the clearing. Tate grinned and waved and Sean hollered, "Hey Ma! Look at my new horse! He's an appaloosa, ain't he purty?"

She waved her good arm and spoke but couldn't be heard over the sound of all the horses tromping through the clearing on their way to the corral at the back of the cabin. Tate wasted no time stripping the animals and turning them free in the corrals for their fresh water from the stream. He walked quickly back to the porch and mounted the steps to look at his wife. He smiled as he bent to give her a kiss and asked Red Hawk, "How'd you get her out here?"

Maggie answered before Red Hawk could and said, "I wrapped my bad arm around her shoulder, used that stick there for a crutch, and hopped. I couldn't stand that bed any longer, I had to sit up! But you're just in time to cook supper!" she smiled mischievously as she looked up at her man.

"That didn't take long!" he answered. "Outta bed a few minutes an' already you're givin' orders!" He sat down beside her and took her hand in his, "But, it sure is good to see you up."

THREE WEEKS PASSED QUICKLY, and Red Hawks ministrations had done their job. Maggie's cuts and bruises were mostly healed, the splints had been changed repeatedly, but still served their purpose and would have to remain for a week or two more, but she was maneuvering quite well. It was late morning when Red Hawk spoke to Maggie, "It is time to return to my village. You do well. Will you come and visit?"

Maggie took Red Hawk's hands in hers and looked to the woman who had become such a good friend and as she said, sister. "Of course, as soon as I'm able to ride, we will all come to see you. I can't thank you enough Red Hawk. There is no way we could have done this without you. Thank you so much."

Red Hawk pulled her close and hugged her friend. As they parted, she handed Maggie a small parcel. Maggie showed surprise and opened the package to reveal a beautiful beaded necklace with a central piece that was of bright yellow, white, and red beads that was a starburst design. Maggie admired the piece and looked to her friend, "Oh, Red Hawk, this is beautiful. Did you make this?"

"Yes. While you sleep, I do beads," she smiled.

Maggie turned around and reached for a leather pouch on the table and handed it to her friend. Red Hawk smiled widely and opened the pouch and reached in to pull out a beautiful silver and turquoise squash blossom necklace. The woman had never seen such a piece and she looked to Maggie and back at the necklace, and Maggie said, "That is made by the Navajo. One of our friends, a Ute woman, traded it from a Navajo and I traded it from her. It is yours now, enjoy."

Red Hawk smiled and put it over her head to drape below her chin and smiled at Maggie, "It is very pretty. I have not seen one before." She smiled as she touched the large piece of turquoise. "I am grateful."

MAGGIE WAS SEATED in her rocker on the porch and Tate stood at the top of the stairs and they waved good bye to their friends as they turned away and started for the trail. Tate sat beside Maggie, took her hand in his and smiled at his beautiful redhead. Sean and Sadie came running from behind the house and scampered up the porch steps, laughing all the while.

"Whoooaaa, what are you two up to?" asked Tate, grabbing Sean and pulling him close as Sadie took her mother's hand to stand beside her.

"Oh, I was just showin' her my new horse. I wanna name him Stardust, cuz o' the spots on his rump. But she thinks I should just call him Spots!"

"Well, I think Stardust is a fine name," said Maggie. "Maybe we can call the mare Spots." She looked to Sadie for approval and the girl nodded her head. Maggie looked

to Tate and he smiled back, as Maggie said, "It's wonderful, isn't it?" and she knew they were both thinking about
their family, their home and their life, as Lobo flopped
down at their feet, not to be ignored.

LOOK FOR RENEGADE RAMPAGE

The next installment in the Rocky Mountain Saint series.